"Saxon, what in heaven's name are you doing?"

Saxon, shirtless, was splitting wood. His back muscles bunched each time he swung the ax, and his skin glistened with sweat. It shocked her to see him doing physical labor. He'd never wanted to help around the ranch. But shock wasn't all. Desire gnawed at her enough to have her clutching her stomach.

Pausing, he spun, saw her and grinned. "I'm cutting wood. What does it look like I'm doing?"

"Why?" Jewell waved a hand aimlessly, more to cool her face than anything.

"The temperature's gonna dip, and it might rain. I figured I'd fill the shed near the house with wood. I left you a message earlier."

"I had a doctor's appointment."

"You did? How did that go?" Burying the blade in the stump, he reached for a T-shirt and rubbed it down his chest.

Jewell's eyes tracked the path of the soft fabric before she blurted, "I'm pregnant. Eight weeks."

Dear Reader,

This is the third and final book in the Snowy Owl Ranchers series. Jewell Hyatt, the local veterinarian, was born and raised in the small Montana community. She and Saxon Conrad met when his parents died and he came to live with his bachelor uncle next door. Uncle and nephew had a long-rocky relationship. Jewell, who always had a crush on Saxon, took his part. She facilitated his interest in writing, singing and performing country music. The crush blossomed into love. But there came a time near the end of college when Saxon's need to go to Nashville and make his mark in the industry conflicted with Jewell's dream of living forever in her hometown. Of being a vet and saving a refuge for the snowy owls.

Saxon and Jewell split up. They meet again when they're older and more entrenched in their chosen fields. Fate and friends take a hand in bringing this couple together a third time. But is it enough even in the Christmas season of miracles to allow them to settle their differences and make a life together?

I welcome hearing from readers via mail at 7739 E. Broadway Blvd #101, Tucson, AZ 85710-3941, email at rdfox@cox.net or via my website, korynna.com/rozfox.

Sincerely,

Roz Denny Fox

A MONTANA CHRISTMAS REUNION

ROZ DENNY FOX

ISBN-13: 978-0-373-75739-8

A Montana Christmas Reunion

This edition published by arrangement with Harlequin Books S.A.

For questions and comments about the quality of this book, please contact us at CustomerService@Harlequin.com.

Printed in U.S.A.

Roz Denny Fox's first book was published by Harlequin in 1990. She writes for several Harlequin lines and her books are published worldwide in a number of languages. Roz's warm home-and-family-focused love stories have been nominated for various industry awards, including the Romance Writers of America's RITA® Award, the Holt Medallion, the Golden Quill and others. Roz has been a member of the Romance Writers of America since 1987 and is currently a member of Tucson's Saguaro Romance Writers, where she has received the Barbara Award for outstanding chapter service. In 2013 Roz received her fifty-book pin from Harlequin. Readers can contact her through Facebook or at rdfox@cox.net, or visit her website at korynna.com/rozfox.

Books by Roz Denny Fox

Harlequin American Romance

The Maverick Returns
Duke: Deputy Cowboy
Texas Dad
Texas Mom

Snowy Owl Ranchers

His Ranch or Hers
A Maverick's Heart

Harlequin Heartwarming

Annie's Neighborhood
An Unlikely Rancher
Molly's Garden

Visit the Author Profile page
at Harlequin.com for more titles.

I'd like to dedicate this story to the National Wildlife Federation. An article in one of their magazines sparked my interest in snowy owls that generally live in the frozen tundra. But due to changing weather and an evaporating food source, they're migrating to Canada and the lower forty-eight. I don't know if they nest in Montana, but as some are being followed in Michigan, my story-owls settled in cold, snowy northeastern Montana.

I'd also like to dedicate this book to Johanna Raisanen, editor, who inherited this project late in the process. My heartfelt gratitude for all of her help.

Chapter One

Jewell Hyatt considered herself fearless. But as she emerged from the airplane at Reagan National, for the first time ever setting foot east of the Missouri River, she was overwhelmed by the crush of people. She reminded herself she'd come to Washington, DC, to convince members of the Natural Resources Committee to authorize a refuge for snowy owls. Focusing, she merged with a stream of travelers rushing to the baggage area.

Her good friend Tawana Whitefeather was supposed to come, too, but she had ended up needing emergency gallbladder surgery. Because it'd taken months to secure the meeting, Jewell had to come alone. She was the owls' biggest advocate—starting at age ten when she'd found a chick with a broken leg who'd blown off course and she'd nursed it back to health.

Oh, boy! If she thought traffic inside the airport was chaotic, driving her rental car in a virtual rabbit warren of whizzing vehicles gave her heartburn.

It was with profound relief that she arrived in one piece at the hotel's parking garage—thanks to her GPS.

After collecting her bag, Jewell checked in.

In her room at last, she toed off her shoes and flopped down on the bed, grateful she had a whole night to unwind before the meeting. While it was the most important part of her trip, the meeting wasn't her only mission. A client had asked her to make a side trip to Maryland to check a stallion and possibly ship sperm home. And fortunately, or unfortunately, depending on her wavering point of view, her closest neighbor had also begged her to hand-deliver a letter to his nephew, who was headlining a nearby country-western concert.

Leland Conrad's request had come as a shock. Given how long he and his nephew had been estranged, Jewell wouldn't have thought he had any idea of Saxon's performance schedule. Saxon had lost both of his parents in a car accident at age twelve. He'd been sent to live with his bachelor uncle, for whom he'd always seemed a burden. And he'd been Jewell's first love.

As memories crowded in, she surged to her feet to go hang a few items in the closet. If only Leland had let her women's group buy his forest to use as an owl refuge, this entire trip would've been unnecessary.

She sank down again, rubbing her temples. Knowing she was a scant few miles from where Saxon Conrad was due to perform made her head ache. But those counting on her to secure a refuge would expect her to be at the top of her game tomorrow instead of mooning over a lost love.

Not lost. She had broken up with Saxon. It shouldn't still affect her. But it did. Maybe seeing him onstage in all his trappings would let her purge him from her soul.

In the morning Jewell collected her notes and checked to be sure she had the credentials the committee had sent her to gain entry into the government building. Her contact recommended taking a cab, so she did.

Once she gave the driver the address, Jewell brought up the weather. "It's awfully cloudy. Is it supposed to rain?"

The cabbie glanced at her. "Are you not tracking Al-thea's progress?"

"Who?"

He laughed. "Our first named Atlantic storm of the season. It's anybody's guess where she'll come ashore, or if she'll be a hurricane. June's early, but lately our weather's been screwy."

"A hurricane?" Feeling like a parrot, Jewell ducked down for a better look at the murky sky. "I was planning to drive to Maryland this afternoon. Should I worry?"

"Listen to advisories." He pulled up to a guarded gate, indicating this was where she should get out.

Rattled by the storm news, Jewell was almost too discombobulated to dig out her phone to take a photo of the Capitol to show her friends in Montana.

A guard checked her pass and handed her off to an intern, who set Jewell at ease as they traversed corri-dors. Once inside the meeting room, she was surprised that instead of everyone being seated around one table, she sat alone facing three men and three women. They were elevated, making her feel a bit on trial. But one woman smiled and, following introductions, invited Jewell to state her case.

"As I explained in emails, our ranch community

was renamed for the snowy owls that migrated to our area. Everyone loves them. Local Native Americans adopted them as a talisman. The man who owns the timber I told you about has his property listed to sell. We worry a buyer may log off the trees, leaving our snowies homeless."

"We expected a tribal representative," said a bespectacled man.

Jewell quickly explained Tawana's absence.

"Sorry," one of the men said. "But you seem to be the owl caretaker."

"Yes, I band chicks and keep a tally. Our owl numbers aren't huge, and of course, the tundra is their normal habitat. I worry about decline."

Members discussed possible reasons, such as mining, logging, changing weather and food depletion, all of which Jewell knew. Then a representative who kept glancing at his watch said, "There's a waterfowl preserve near you. Just relocate the owls."

"They settled of their own accord in abandoned eagles' nests or atop boulders. The lake isn't close. Like I said, the owner of the land where they live wants to sell. If you'd purchase that portion as a refuge, my friends and I will gladly maintain it."

The members glanced awkwardly at one another. The chairwoman closed her notebook. "I'm sorry, Dr. Hyatt. We thought your group had land. We post privately owned parcels or work with wildlife defenders who buy areas that we then make federal reserves."

"We have some funds. Far from enough to buy Conrad's ranch. And he's not inclined to divide his property for us. We hoped your leverage…" She didn't finish as all the members shook their heads.

"It's too bad he won't work with you," a man said. Others rose and began leaving. The chairwoman waited. "I'll have one of our wildlife biologists inspect your nesting site when he's out west. We're aware snowies are migrating and adapting. In fact, we're following a group in Michigan. I'll email you a list of birder groups to contact." With that she opened the door and called the intern to escort Jewell out.

Numb with disappointment, Jewell trudged out. Why hadn't the person she'd emailed with told her this? It would've saved money and time spent on this useless trip.

Out on the street she caught a cab. Frankly, she was so disheartened she wanted to catch the next flight home. But she'd promised Mark Watson she'd check the stallion. And while more than ever she'd prefer to skip Saxon's concert, it was probably not the time to let Leland down.

Not until after she changed into clothes suitable to visit the horse farm did Jewell remember her first cab driver's warning about the weather. It was one o'clock. The sky looked the same. She took a moment to phone Tawana to share the bad news and see how her friend was doing.

"I hope I'll be released from the hospital tomorrow. Gosh, Jewell, I can hear how upset you are. When you return, let's call the Artsy Ladies together and figure out a next step. Hey, I saw on TV that DC may get socked by a hurricane. Are you in danger?"

"It's not certain where or when the storm will land. Don't worry."

"Okay, be careful."

Jewell said goodbye and turned on the TV as she donned her boots. A local station showed three places the storm might make landfall. But they said Althea had slowed and it'd probably be midnight before she came ashore.

Jewell snagged her jean jacket, then hurried to the parking garage to reclaim her rental. She hadn't driven far before she fervently wished for the wide-open spaces of home. However, once she reached Maryland, the countryside became awash with fields of lush grass and white rail fences, and she relaxed.

But even with a GPS, she somehow got off on a wrong freeway and ended up in West Virginia. She had to stop and phone the owner of the horse farm. Thankfully, he provided her better directions.

As it turned out, the owner and his wife were delightful. They had beautiful horses. Jewell had completed ordering the sperm sent to Mark when the owner mentioned the hurricane.

"Montana gets a lot of wind and snow, but I've never been close to a hurricane."

The owner's wife checked the weather on her cell phone and told Jewell the storm was spinning offshore. The couple assured her she'd have ample time to drive back to DC.

Jewell didn't volunteer that she was making a side trip about an hour away. Perhaps the storm warnings were telling her she should skip Saxon's concert. But Leland had paid for her ticket.

Stopped at a crossroad, Jewell studied the blustery sky. She didn't know how much of the pewter color was due to the late hour and how much to an impending storm. She snapped on the radio. A woman said the hurricane had stalled. A man interrupted to say it had gathered strength. Nothing in their banter sounded so dire to Jewell that it would hurt her to swing by the town hosting the concert. If reports worsened, she could run in and give Leland's letter to someone associated with Saxon and hurry back to her hotel.

After meandering for another hour through horse country, Jewell spotted the rustic theater advertising Saxon's concert on its marquee.

Not detecting any change in the weather, she paid to park in a lot a block away but didn't immediately get out. Her stomach churned at the prospect of seeing Saxon. Probably it was good that she'd skipped lunch.

Even now she had trouble understanding how she and Saxon had gone from best friends to lovers to virtual strangers. She'd followed his career for a while, until she began to see him paired with a pretty blonde singer. Only then did she date. She had even briefly been engaged to the son of a local rancher. But there was no spark, so she'd returned his ring.

Gripping the steering wheel, she hung on tight. From the time Saxon arrived in Snowy Owl Crossing, they'd been inseparable. She was his shoulder to lean on. He and his uncle constantly clashed. She always took Saxon's side. And he had spent every minute he could at her home. It was where he developed a love of music. Her dad had owned a guitar. Saxon spotted it and spent hours teaching himself to play, often missing chores his uncle gave him.

Jewell had always had a crush on Saxon. She'd been the one to first convince him to play and sing for friends. Later she found him gigs at county fairs and rodeos—anything to keep him in her sphere and give him a break from Leland's nagging him to knuckle down on the ranch.

Looking back with more clarity than she'd had when they'd split, Jewell realized it shouldn't have shocked her to learn near college graduation that nothing on earth could entice Saxon to return to his uncle's. Not even her.

Maybe if she hadn't been so single-minded, so deep in her own studies and plans for the future, she'd have anticipated how it'd end when he left agriculture and switched to a music track.

The awful truth didn't register until he announced that he was going to Nashville. He assumed she'd go along to support him. He even said once he signed with a label, she could enroll in vet school in Tennessee. But Nashville wasn't Snowy Owl Crossing, and Tennessee wasn't Montana. Looking back, she saw it was obvious their love hadn't been strong enough.

Rain began striking her windshield. Jewell released her death grip on the steering wheel and found a tissue to blot her tears.

Assuming she wouldn't get close enough to Saxon to hand him Leland's letter, she figured she could ask someone on his staff to deliver it. She'd come this far.

And a sick man back home counted on her. At least, Doreen Mercer, who owned the café and kept tabs on Leland, claimed he wasn't well.

Dashing to the theater, Jewell dug out her ticket. She was maneuvered into a line of noisy people filtered between two sets of velvet ropes.

Making sure the letter hadn't fallen out of her purse, she peered around two women directly in front of her and her breath stuck in her throat. Saxon stood up ahead cordoned off by the left rope. He appeared to be greeting concertgoers, thanking them for coming and handing out T-shirts bearing his likeness.

Panic gripped Jewell. She should flee before she made a spectacle of herself and fainted or threw up. But she was hemmed in by the boisterous crowd. The line inched forward. Everyone wanted to speak to Saxon. Most wanted his autograph.

Jewell forced herself to think. This could be her chance to hand over Leland's letter, duck under the rope and escape. Except her feet wouldn't move, and she pawed in her purse and couldn't find the letter. Nor could she take her eyes off Saxon. He looked the same yet different. He'd shot up to six feet early in his teens, but he used to be runner thin. Now he had filled out nicely in his chest and shoulders. While his dark hair had always had a slight curl, tonight it looked wonderfully mussed. *Probably styled.*

Admittedly, she'd viewed him online a few times. But, wow, he was way more potent in person. So darned good-looking it played havoc with her vow to see him in the trappings of his trade and once and for all…flush him from her system.

The woman behind Jewell nudged her to close the gap between herself and the folks in front of her, who had reached Saxon. Paralyzed, she let herself be shoved.

Because she hadn't located the letter, she bent her head to find it and quickly scoot past Saxon to where helpers ushered ticket holders into the theater. The letter stubbornly evaded her search. Suddenly she had no time left. Should she rush by, let someone seat her and ask an usher to deliver the letter?

"Jewell? Jewell Hyatt, my God!"

Hearing her name breathed out quietly but reverently had her lifting her head. Her gaze locked with Saxon's silvery-gray eyes. First disbelief spread over his handsome face; then something akin to joy made heat flood her belly. "Hello, Saxon." Her greeting sounded high and strained but was all she could manage.

"What are you doing here?" He ignored staffers who were trying to move Jewell and those behind her through the line faster.

"I…ah…came on business. Uh…Leland asked me to bring you a letter." She bent and fumbled again inside her purse in earnest.

"Leland? Who cares?" Saxon said gruffly.

Jewell glanced up in time to see a hefty man to Saxon's right poke him and mutter, "Boss, we need to move folks along. Some are still stuck out in the rain."

Nodding, Saxon raised a hand and signaled a man standing at the end of the velvet ropes. "Donovan! Hey, Donovan!"

That man rushed up.

Saxon indicated Jewell. "She's an old friend. Seat her in VIP."

Even though Jewell had the letter half out by then, the man in the dark blue Western-style suit propelled her briskly into the hall. She almost dropped her purse and the T-shirt Saxon had given her before he recognized her and set up a fuss she didn't want or need.

"Really, this isn't necessary," she said when they ended up standing by the first row, which was within spitting distance of the stage.

"Saxon wants you here." Leaning over, the man unhooked a gold rope, then pressed her into the first of six empty plush seats. He adeptly reattached the rope, straightened and stood at the end of the row with feet apart and hands tucked behind his back like a military guard.

Jewell sensed eyes boring into her back. She felt on display because this short set of seats was separated from the longer row behind by eight or ten feet of empty space. This was too much. She felt imprisoned, and why? She yanked out Leland's letter, zipped her purse and started to ask her apparent jailer to deliver it before insisting she had to leave. But as she rose from her seat, a younger guy pulled Donovan aside and began gesturing and whispering. Then he departed through a side door to the left of the stage.

Waving the letter, Jewell attracted Donovan's attention. "I came here primarily to give Saxon a letter from his uncle. I'm from Saxon's hometown. Frankly, I don't know why his uncle didn't mail this. Maybe Saxon travels too much," she offered lamely.

"Keep it. I have orders to take you backstage after the performance. Lance just said it may be a short concert due to the hurricane landing sooner than expected."

"Heavens, then I really need to give you this and go. I have to drive back to my hotel in DC." She managed to unhook the gold rope but dropped the letter. She bent to retrieve it, but Donovan scooped it up and tucked it in his suit-coat pocket as the lights dimmed and blinked twice and a disembodied voice from above asked everyone to take their seats. "The concert begins in two minutes."

Stepping over the rope, Donovan scooted Jewell into the adjacent seat, and after growling, "Stay," which reminded her of how one would address a dog, he plopped his big body into the seat she'd just vacated.

A hush fell over the theater. Overhead lights went lower still, this time to a muted golden glow. All at once blinding spotlights in multiple colors pinged around a stage where a small band now appeared holding various instruments.

Jewell didn't want to feel eager, but it was the only way to describe the flutter of anticipation that clutched her. And when Saxon bounded onto the stage with guitar in hand, she was transported back to watching him emerge in similar fashion to perform so many times in the past. She'd loved him then. Now she was starstruck. He exuded a commanding presence as he stepped to the front of the stage, smiled and clipped the leather strap of an acoustic guitar around his neck. The audience went wild.

After he'd strummed a few chords, his gray eyes found Jewell. His smile softened momentarily but then hardened. In that first moment, the love she'd so desperately tried to stamp out flooded back, filling her with a desire to return to the past where their connection had been simple and natural and—she'd assumed—forever.

Chapter Two

Someone slid a stool onstage. Saxon half sat on it and then began to play and sing. Jewell, who used to believe he had a good voice, sat mesmerized. His voice had deepened and mellowed. If he still wrote the songs he sang, as he'd done back when she was his primary cheerleader, his lyrics now were decidedly more emotional.

It'd been a long time since she'd seen him perform in person. Never since he'd become famous. After the first time she'd heard him on the radio, she had blocked the pain by telling herself she was too busy to listen to music anyway. Because her work required short jaunts between ranches, it wasn't worth turning on her pickup radio. But if she were being totally honest—country music had always been her favorite, and frankly, she'd been afraid if she heard Saxon singing any of his early tunes, she'd start blubbering.

She was near to weeping now.

She began to wonder about this song that dealt with loneliness and suppressed love, or lost love. Had she ripped apart Saxon's heart? After all, she'd been the one to break things off—to surgically end their relationship.

At twenty-one, she never thought he would have ever expected her to realign her life to follow him. Everyone who knew her knew being a vet in Snowy Owl Crossing was what she'd planned and prepared to do from the time she was old enough to dream.

Now, listening to Saxon's voice grow thick on a chorus about broken promises, Jewell trembled under his almost icy scrutiny. It was patently obvious that he had zeroed in on her. Was he taunting her? It seemed not to matter how tense his jaw was—his voice remained seductive. She was carried back to college days when he'd sung her parts of new songs, and it had frequently ended with their making love.

Uncomfortable, she shifted in her seat. But noting a hush fall over the crowd, she turned slightly to glance behind her. A row of women stared openly at her with envy, because as Saxon began his next number, it couldn't be more evident that he sang the love song to her.

All at once a photographer who'd been taking pictures of Saxon and his band suddenly knelt and snapped off a battery of her. Blinded, Jewell jerked aside. And she worried about where those photos might appear and what they might reveal on her face—the rapture, the love she hadn't been able to completely abolish.

Listening as he crooned her name, she felt her nervousness increase tenfold. Partway into the second verse, she thought, *Phew!* There was no way the people in the audience could know that the jewel he mentioned—like a vibrant diamond he longed for—was her. Only she was aware how many times in the past he'd kissed her and jokingly called her his million-dollar gem. At least, she used to assume it was a joke because they'd laughed together.

More uneasy, she flipped up her jacket collar to hide her burning face. Why was Saxon doing this? He hadn't held her in years. He hadn't called or tried to contact her. And she was quite sure he hadn't been a monk since they'd parted.

Relief washed over her when the song ended—enough for her to actually relax as Saxon announced that he would sing his latest hit next.

Concertgoers clapped and shouted. Some whistled catcalls. But Saxon had barely run a thumb over his guitar's strings when the man who'd first introduced him burst onstage through the back curtains. Grabbing the microphone, he said, "I'm sorry to tell you all, but the hurricane has reportedly made landfall, bringing bands of heavy rain. We need to cancel the rest of the show. As we told each of you at the outset, Saxon and his band appreciate how so many of you ventured out given the unsettled predictions for Althea. Unfortunately, we hear many streets are flooding, which has taken officials by surprise. I spoke with local authorities, who suggest you go home if you live nearby or seek accommodations in this city for tonight. Local motels will offer discounts if you show them your concert ticket stub. Everyone, please take care. And we're sorry. Staff will give each of you a free CD at the door."

Behind her, Jewell heard gasps and the sound of feet

retreating up the aisles. She stood, intending to follow. Donovan leaped up to talk to another man. Suddenly he glanced around and beckoned her.

"Please remember to give Saxon the letter. Tell him I enjoyed the show but I have to go."

The man blocked her exit. "Saxon is waiting for you backstage."

"You don't understand. I need to see about a room, because it sounded as if I'd be foolish to try and drive back to my hotel in DC until this storm passes."

"Watching the stampede of folks out of here, you'd be wise to let someone on Saxon's team secure accommodations for you." Then without waiting for her to agree or object, he clasped her upper arm and all but dragged her through a set of black velvet curtains near the stage. Saxon's band had already cleared out with their instruments.

He stood in a hallway gesturing and talking to a couple of those same band members. Donovan whisked her along, barely letting her boots touch the floor. He didn't stop until her shoulder jostled Saxon's upper arm. "One lady friend delivered as ordered," the man announced.

It didn't surprise her to hear Saxon huff out an exasperated-sounding, "She's an old friend, not some item I ordered off a menu." As if to make a point, he swept her up and swung her around until excitement built inside Jewell like it had when they used to ride the Tilt-A-Whirl at the county fair. Then he unceremoniously plopped her down and went on talking to a young man holding a guitar.

Her stomach had yet to settle when Saxon again

skewered Donovan with a glance. "Speaking of menu, I'm starved. Ask Carson to see if he can scare up a decent meal for two and deliver it to my bus before this town drops its shutters?"

"I can't stay, Saxon. I need to call around and find a room," Jewell said.

Her comment had Saxon frowning down at her.

The last band members moved on out a back door. When it opened, Jewell felt a damp wind *whish* along the hall. Courtesy of an outside light above that same door, she noticed rain flying in circles. "The weather is definitely worse. I wonder how far away hotels or motels are."

Donovan acknowledged Saxon's request for food. Then he, too, rushed out, calling loudly to the absent Carson. Suddenly she and Saxon were the only ones left in a theater where the few lights still burning began going dark one at a time.

His arm tightened around her waist. "Damn, it's really you! Believe it or not, you come to mind so often I first thought I imagined you standing in line. I'm sorry I didn't have a minute before the show to do more than have Donovan find you a seat. This is only the second time we've had to shorten a show due to weather. However, our booking agent is responsible for battening down the hatches, so to speak. Come, we'll have a drink, wait for the food and catch up in my bus. It's parked out back."

Anchoring Jewell more firmly to his side, he moved them along the almost dark hall to shove open a door that seemed to stick. Once they emerged, driving rain and a battering wind jammed Jewell's protest down her throat. "Seriously, Saxon. I'm not kidding about needing to locate a room."

Hunching his larger body around her, Saxon made a hard left turn and plowed on through fat raindrops striking them from all sides.

As the wind robbed her ability to speak, Jewell was unable to object when Saxon keyed some numbers into a pad near the front of a big, dark bus, then opened a door where steps magically appeared. She blinked water from her eyelashes after he rushed them in out of what was definitely deteriorating weather.

Saxon flipped switches until light fell from a series of wall sconces. That gave Jewell time to gather her jumbled senses enough to examine the interior of a vehicle that for all the world looked like a luxury apartment.

He dashed off, leaving her standing behind plush driver and passenger seats. She dripped on real tile that served as a foyer to a living room outfitted with thick beige-colored carpet. Saxon reappeared with two towels, one of which he offered her.

She set her handbag and the now-soaked free T-shirt on a side table and blotted her face and hair with the terrycloth towel. The hem of her shirt not covered by her jacket was also soaked. The hand towels wouldn't do much to dry either of them.

"Saxon, I would love to have time to share a meal, but considering the number of people at the theater who'll be stuck in town, I really need to find accommodations. My hotel is in the heart of DC. I intended to return there after your show, but now that's out of the question." Wadding the towel, she clutched it nervously in front of her.

"Are you afraid of me?" Saxon abruptly asked.

"What? No!"

"It looks like it from the way you're holding that towel like a shield."

Jewell scowled at the object and quickly relaxed her arms. "Here." She tried to pass the towel back. "Donovan said you'd have an assistant find someplace for me to spend the night. Is there someone who'll do that?"

A sharp rap at the door kept Saxon from taking the towel or responding. Before he reached the door, it flew open. A man dressed in a clear slicker gestured to Saxon by holding up two square takeout boxes. "I hope you guys like lasagna. The only restaurant open was an Italian place. Even they were closing up. And Donovan said your friend needed a room. I'm sorry, Sax, but two of us phoned around and couldn't find even an empty broom closet."

Saxon handed Jewell his wet towel so he could accept the boxes from the poor dripping fellow. "Uh, thanks, Carson. Were you able to buy enough to feed you guys and the band?"

"Yeah, the restaurant owner was happy to have me take all remaining pizzas off his hands. If this is all you need, boss, I'd like to get back before the others demolish it."

"By all means. And double thanks for braving the weather."

The response was muffled as the other man shut the door with a loud bang that made Jewell jump.

Facing Jewell again, Saxon shrugged. "You heard him. Maybe the storm will pass quickly. I'm sure you heard me say earlier that I'm starved. Unless you're full up, follow me to the table and I'll serve this while it's hot. My kitchen and dining table are in the center of the coach."

The aroma from the food wafted up, causing Jewell's stomach to growl loudly.

Saxon smiled for the first time since they were left alone together. "That sounds as if you're plenty hungry, too."

"Embarrassing but true. I went to examine a stallion Mark Watson wants to mate with his new mare. I got lost and missed lunch. Where shall I put these towels? They're too wet to set on any of your nice wood furniture." Looking around, she noted the cozy living room and its big-screen TV.

"The kitchen counters are granite. Drop the towels there. If you want, you can wash up at the sink while I grab plates and utensils. So you came across country to check on a horse for Watson? Remember Rafe Laughlin? He came to one of my shows a few years ago. He said you were engaged. Was it to Watson?"

"Mark is older and happily married. I made this trip to speak to the Natural Resources Committee about buying a portion of Leland's land as a snowy owl refuge." Trailing in his wake, Jewell laid the towels on the countertop. "Wow, this is fancy. I had no idea buses could be so swanky." She swept a hand around to take in stainless-steel appliances that included a dishwasher and wine fridge. She noticed it only because after setting out plates, napkins and silverware, Saxon got out a bottle of wine. Holding it out for her to see the label, he pulled the cork. "Do you still prefer chardonnay regardless of what type of food is served?"

Jewell saw it was a brand they sometimes used to buy as a treat after acing their college tests. Almost as quickly, she recalled if they indulged too much, their evenings usually ended in a sleepover. Back then not a lot of sleeping went on. "I…still do prefer chardonnay. But only one glass with dinner. Hopefully, I'll get to drive back to DC later."

"Doubtful from the sound of that wind." He set aside the cork and poured wine into two glasses. "Let's sit and fill our plates. Then you can catch me up on what's happening in the lives of the old home crowd." Pausing, he studied her. "I still can't believe you're here. If you only knew how many times I spotted someone with hair the color of yours in the crowd and my heart… Well, suffice to say, until tonight I was always wrong and disappointed."

Having no idea how to respond, Jewell dipped her head and slid into a chair across the table from him. Opening her food carton, she sniffed the pungent garlic scent. "This looks and smells fantastic. Can we eat first and talk after I appease my empty stomach?"

Chuckling, Saxon scooped lasagna onto his plate, along with asparagus and two slices of toasted garlic bread. "I can't say I'm sorry the only restaurant open was Italian. Remember that little hole-in-the-wall place near campus that served the world's best spaghetti and meatballs? I recall it every time I eat Italian food."

Jewell smiled and felt the knot in her stomach ease. "Rossiano's. Good food and cheap. I wonder if it's still there. I have to admit I rarely get out of Snowy Owl Crossing these days."

"Yet here you are." Saxon picked up his wineglass and took a drink. Setting it down, he said, "You mentioned asking a committee to buy some of Uncle Leland's land. Is he selling out? If so, I suppose he wants a fortune."

"His Realtor advised him not to break up the ranch, which includes the area where owls nest." After blotting red sauce off her lips, Jewell set her napkin back on her lap. "My meeting with the federal committee didn't go as I'd hoped." Between bites, she launched into an explanation of the efforts already put forth by the Artsy Ladies. "One member of the national committee said maybe we can partner with a birder group to buy the land."

"Who are the Artsy Ladies?"

Jewell named them. "We all make and sell crafts. We hope the money will one day buy land for a snowy owl refuge."

"Okay, I know most everyone. I'm drawing a blank on Myra Maxwell."

"Until this past spring she was Myra Odell. Remember she only spent summers with her grandparents? Her grandmother passed and Myra moved to Snowy Owl Crossing to run the ranch the last three years. Then her grandfather died."

"Now I can place her. I'm sorry to hear about the

Odells. You say Myra married someone named Maxwell? That name doesn't ring any bells."

"It's quite a story. Myra's dad gave the ranch to Zeke Maxwell, an ex-military guy who saved her brother's life. Myra and Zeke fell in love and married. They run the Flying Owl now. Zeke has a twin, Seth. Before I left home, I sensed he and Lila Jenkins will be the next in our group to walk down the aisle."

"Lila? Did she and Keith divorce?" Saxon paused in eating and frowned. "Rafe didn't mention anyone but you when we talked. He travels a lot selling farm equipment. Sometime after college he left Montana for Tulsa."

"You really are behind times." She glossed over the horrific mine accident in which Keith and other miners died.

"Gosh, I'm sorry to hear it. I remember they got married right out of high school. And didn't they have a son about the time we graduated from college?"

"Yes. Rory is nine. He's nuts about playing baseball, something Seth Maxwell's been helping with. Actually, another of Zeke's groomsmen, a guy who lost a leg in Afghanistan, kinda fell for Tawana. We expect he'll move back when he's done with rehab at the VA. They all fit well into the community." She ate a few bites to let Saxon absorb all she'd said.

"In my mind things in Snowy Owl Crossing remain as they were when I left. Obviously not."

"You could've caught up if you'd bothered to touch base with anyone," Jewell said pointedly.

He idly broke apart a slice of garlic bread. "I had a

tough time believing we were through, Jewell. You were my rock. The constant in my life."

"Your only living relative is still in town, Saxon. Leland is aging," she chided softly. "He looks poorly but doesn't complain. At least, not to me. What did he have to say in the letter I brought?"

"You didn't give me a letter."

"Donovan took it. I planned to leave when the show ended. Your uncle didn't share what he wrote, but he was anxious enough to bribe me to hand-deliver it. He paid for my ticket to your show." She finished off her wine.

Filling their glasses again, Saxon paused, his eyebrows diving together. "Donovan will give me the letter next time I see him. But I don't want to talk about my uncle. You, of all people, know he's why I had to leave Snowy Owl Crossing."

Jewell moved her plate so she could set her elbows on the table. "I know he seemed detached and hard on you as a kid. People can change, Saxon," she said, propping her chin on folded hands. "It's not healthy to hold a grudge so long."

"You haven't held one against me?"

"What? No. Do you not know how shocked I was to learn we had such conflicting goals? I assumed we would..." She lowered her eyes. "Plainly, back then we were both naive. I've often wondered how you're doing," she murmured, picking up her wine.

"Yeah. You probably hoped I'd fail and have to return to Montana." He took a long drink from his glass.

"What a horrible thing to say. With your talent, I knew you'd succeed."

"I almost didn't. My first five years in Nashville were a hand-to-mouth struggle to get anyone to hear a demo. All I wanted was to live up to your expectations. I owe you so much but have no idea how to repay you."

"I don't want to be repaid for anything, Saxon. I wanted us both to have our careers. I'm sorry we lost touch."

"Really? I phoned your mom during one of my lowest periods. You were off at veterinary school in Washington State."

"You talked to Mom? She never told me."

"Yes, well, she never came right out and said it was best I forget you, but it was implied. And once I got my head screwed on straight enough to admit you deserved to be the hometown vet, I focused all my energy on making my music work. I stuck it out even when I lived in a dive of an apartment and couldn't afford to feed myself."

Jewell bit her lip. "I'm sorry. I didn't have any idea your life was so hard." She indicated the room with a wave of one hand. "I'd say things have picked up."

"I suppose I should thank you for dumping me. Had you gone with me to Nashville, there's no way I could've made a go of my music and paid for you to attend vet school like I promised."

She took a drink, then swirled the wine. "I'd like to say I was smart enough to see that. Closer to the truth, I was crushed when you made clear you could never live in Snowy Owl Crossing. Not even for me." She finished the wine and set down her empty glass.

"If it means anything, I never got you out of my system. I hung on to the fact that your mother said you were happy." Leaning forward, Saxon took her hands, which forced her to stare straight into his somber gray eyes.

As if stuck in a dream, she squeezed his warm hands. But eventually she pulled hers free. "That's bullshit, Saxon. Remote as we are, we have cell towers. Once when I was surfing the web, I ran across photos of you with a cute little blonde singer. There was speculation that you two planned to marry."

"Marry? I've dated, but never got engaged like you apparently did. But I can't think… Ah, you must mean Toni French. We had the same agent and recording label for a while. They splash all that hype around because fans love what they believe is access into recording artists' private lives. Toni and I were never romantically involved. In fact, she moved to a different label. Are you saying you cared?"

Jewell shrugged. "I figured you'd gotten married and maybe even divorced like so many performers."

"Did you?"

"Did I what?" She thought she'd missed something because his forehead was furrowed again.

"You aren't wearing a wedding ring, but Rafe said he heard you were engaged. Have you married and divorced? If so, to anyone I know?"

That last part of his query sounded testy enough for Jewell to slowly shake her head, just feeling sad. "My engagement was brief. Now I'm too busy to date. But it's pointless for us to travel this path, Saxon. I'll help you clear the table and then try to find a place to stay. Or if the storm's abated, I'll return to my hotel." The last had barely left her lips when wind rocked the bus and they could hear bands of rain striking the metal siding.

Saxon got up to peer out a window. He dropped the curtain and dug a cell phone out of his pocket. "It's too dark to see much. But the wind is definitely tossing stuff around." He pushed a few buttons on his phone. "Althea's now listed as a strong tropical storm packing heavy rain and high winds. No way will I let you drive anywhere in these conditions. You can sleep here."

Jewell's heart did a little flip as she recalled how even when they were kids, Saxon had looked out for her safety and well-being. "How long before it'll be over?"

He scrolled more. "Wee hours of the morning."

She watched him return his stare to her, and she unconsciously licked her lips as their history kept playing over and over in her head. Trying to shake off the memories, she found her voice. "I trust this luxury conveyance has two bedrooms."

"Nope. One bed almost fills the only bedroom. It could sleep four. I have any number of oversize T-shirts I can lend you. We'll have to pretend it's old times."

As Jewell mulled over his offer to share a bed, he added, "How many times did we study so late we made do crammed together in one narrow dorm bed?"

"That was a long time ago."

"For me those years melted away the minute I laid eyes on you. Can you honestly say seeing me hasn't triggered some wistful feelings in you?"

She gave a slow shake of her head. “The music…” Her voice cracked and she stood. “When did you write songs for me, Saxon?”

He grew serious again. “I’ve written a few with you in mind.” Brushing her bangs aside with the backs of his fingers, he curved one hand around the side of her neck. Bending, he kissed her. Softly at first, but he continued kissing her with more fervor until both her hands slid up and down his chest and finally she clamped her hands over his shoulders.

The coach swayed in the wind, but the air Jewell breathed felt hot and sultry. Yes, she remembered loving him, loving his kisses. She might have been a girl back then, but she’d loved him like a woman. The good times they’d had tumbled over and over in fond memories that ran together in a blur. It didn’t take long for the old excitement to flutter in her belly and she wanted him with every fiber of her being.

He picked her up as if even in boots, jeans and a jacket she were feather light. Some small slice of her brain said she should object to being carried down a dim hall into a dark room. Then he sat with her on his lap, and their kisses went on until Jewell thought she’d go mad unless she touched his skin and he touched hers. She made the first move, ripping open the snaps down the front of his Western-style shirt.

“Whoa, whoa!” Saxon pulled back. He sucked in a breath. “Let’s have some light and lose enough clothes to get comfortable.”

Jewell blinked even though the bedside lamp he snapped on was little more than an amber glow. His hands had always been strong but seemed more so now as he removed her boots and set them beneath a bedside chair.

Because her bones were limp as cooked noodles, and because she drowned in his crooked smile, she had nothing to say when her damp jacket and wrinkled shirt landed on the chair. Suffused in heat, she still shivered when Saxon strung soft kisses from below her ear down her torso, stopping at the V of her bra. Dazedly, she ran her hands over the sculpted muscles of his back.

"I hate like the devil to interrupt what we've got going, but I need to make a quick check in the bathroom to see if my agent stocked, uh…protection."

Rising, he placed a finger over Jewell's trembling lips. "Before you get all huffy and ask why Sid would do that? Agents just do. They assume all performers meet and fall into bed with groupies. Some do. I don't. But agents and managers are charged with making sure the label doesn't get sued. No matter how many times I've said I only want Tylenol, soap and aftershave, Sid puts a packet or two in my medicine cabinet. Be right back." And he disappeared.

In the respite Jewell tried to clear her head. What flashed there like a neon sign was a niggling thought that spending a night making love with Saxon probably wasn't smart. But even as she sat alone, she burned with desire for him. Wants and needs she hadn't felt in a long time clouded her vision and made mush of her brain. Really, he was the only one who'd ever made her feel this way.

Saxon returned and handed her a crumpled foil

packet and a T-shirt. "Maybe Sid finally got my message. I found one condom." He sat at her side and caressed her cheek. "You're still wearing way too many clothes." He knelt to slowly peel away her jeans.

Jewell saw all he wore on his lean, tanned body was a pair of navy briefs. She could have admired the view longer, but he sank down beside her and tipped up her face, and she again grew weak from his kisses.

Beyond, in the tail of the coach, the wind whistled. Feeling pulled into the vortex of the storm, Jewell wedged a space. "Give me a minute in the bathroom, please."

"By all means. Lights or no lights tonight?"

"I haven't changed that much," she said.

He studied her without blinking. "Darkness it is, even if I want to see every beautiful inch of you."

She scurried into the opulent bathroom. Her heart slammed erratically in her chest as she stood for a moment clutching the T-shirt that smelled of the woodsy, smoky sandalwood scent that still always had her looking around for Saxon in the café or at a rodeo. Quickly she slipped on his large T-shirt, but wondered if she was being foolish. The pull of not knowing left her jittery, but eager.

Only a faint light from the living room sconces that Saxon had left on guided her into his open arms. How often over the years had she awakened from a dream to a vivid memory of this man's delicious exploration of her body? Too many times to count, but she'd never admit that to him.

Soon he drove her to a fevered pitch, let her sink and

drove her up again until she shattered around him. Jewell curled into him and whispered against his muscular chest, "You haven't lost your touch."

His pleasure at her comment was reflected in how snugly he wrapped her in his arms. "You complete me, Jewell. You always have. The music used to be enough, but lately I've wanted…more."

What did he mean? Was he ready to put down roots in Snowy Owl Crossing? Molding her cheek to his toasty skin, she yawned. "Uh-um," she murmured sleepily.

"Monday I have a four-day gig in Nashville, then head into a month-long tour across the South and Southwest. We end in LA for a benefit where a host of recording stars are raising money to fight against world hunger. Come with me."

"Wha…hat?" She lifted her head slightly.

"I mean it. I make good money now. And you're an experienced veterinarian who can hang her shingle anywhere. If you'd prefer, we can give living together a try before doing anything permanent. How does that sound?"

"Like I'm fuzzy headed from too much wine." Unable to sort out his comments, she yawned bigger and tightened her arm across his chest.

His chuckle was a low rumble in her ear. She nodded when he proposed they sleep on it and talk again in the morning.

Saxon fell asleep almost immediately. But in spite of how tired Jewell was, she lay listening to him breathe, timing the sound to wind that eventually stopped buffeting the coach. She battled still loving him against a sick feeling that while he hadn't discounted her career like before, he ignored her love for Snowy Owl Crossing. Ignored that she had a life and fulfilling career there. Really, nothing had changed except they were older. He no longer struggled to make ends meet, and she should be happy to tag along.

Very close to crying yet not wanting to wake him, she slid out of bed. Wishing badly that things could be different but knowing it wasn't possible, she silently gathered her clothes and tiptoed down the hall to dress under the soft living room lighting. She looked around for something on which to scribble him a note. A few business cards sat on the coffee table. Holding one under a sconce, she saw it belonged to Saxon's agent, Sid Andrews. She stuck one in her purse for Leland. She'd have to trust Donovan would give Saxon his uncle's letter. But from the way Saxon balked at discussing his uncle, that'd probably be the end of it.

She turned over another card and wrote, "It's roundup time at home. And I'm scheduled as the vet for the July Fourth rodeo. Sorry." She scribbled a *J*. Really, what else could she say? Surely he'd see it was the storm, the wine and memories that got to them. Casting a last look around his chosen home, she slipped out into a predawn that smelled of recent rain.

She ran through the parking lot, and it wasn't until she reached her rental car that she breathed again.

Sniffling away tears, she listened to the disembodied voice from the GPS. It crossed her mind how much better her life would be if she could stop crying over Saxon Conrad.

Chapter Three

Saxon woke up feeling more rested than he had in longer than he could remember. Rested and smiling—a huge deal for someone who wasn't a morning person. He stretched and suddenly remembered why he was happy. Jewell had come back into his life.

Rolling over, he reached for her, but his arm swept cool, empty space.

Assuming she was in the kitchen, he swung out of bed. And dang it all, when he'd drifted off to sleep after their fantastic hour of lovemaking, his plan had been to fix her breakfast.

It wasn't pitch-black in the bedroom. Enough light filtered through the window blinds that he was able to see the chair where Jewell had stacked her clothes was empty.

Thoughts of the storm that had caused the cancellation of his show and that was responsible for Jewell spending the night flooded back into his foggy morning brain. His feet tangled in his undershorts, which had ended up on the floor. For propriety's sake, he donned them and even stopped to grab his jeans from the hook on the back of his bathroom door. If he didn't have a guest, he'd as likely tramp off buck naked to make coffee.

Unless Jewell had totally changed, she was someone who needed caffeine prior to saying good morning.

He came out of the bathroom and sniffed the air. No coffee smell. And the bus seemed too still. Panic gripped him as he sped down the hall. Had he dreamed the whole encounter with Jewell? It wouldn't be the first time. But never before had holding her, kissing her, loving her seemed so real.

The kitchen was empty. He snapped on the light. Last night had been real. The remains of two dinners were proof.

Stifling a yawn, he noticed a faint light shone from the living room. Maybe Jewell had gone there to keep from waking him.

All wall sconces burned, but the room was empty. From there he could see out through the wide bus windshield. What was visible of the sky was streaked with lavender and pink, a sign the storm had passed. His bus sat behind one used by his band. It would shock him to see any sign of life there this early.

He clutched a railing that separated the bus driver from his living area. He'd had the wall that came with the bus removed because he and the band often jammed on the road or planned concerts. Ducking, he ran his gaze along the street that went behind the theater. The asphalt gleamed with wet puddles, but nothing moved for as far as he could see in any direction.

Jewell had gone. She'd left without a word. Last night

he'd invited her to travel with him—again. She'd slunk away in the night like a thief—one who'd made off with his heart. He'd spent years trying to forget her. Last night she'd shown up and suddenly he was back where he'd started—when he'd loved her with every fiber of his being.

He stumbled to the couch, dropped down and buried his head in his hands.

Hours later he remained there when someone rapped on his door. Because Donovan had the code, he waltzed right in. "Hey, what's up?" He climbed the two steps. "Rough night? You look like hell." He swiveled his big body around. "Where's your lady friend? Should I pipe down? Is she still asleep?"

Saxon dragged his hands down his face and felt the prickle of whiskers. "She left."

"It's just as well. I'm surprised she joined you. She almost bolted before the concert started and again when it got canceled." He extracted a folded envelope from the inside pocket of his suit coat. "Who is she? Last night she asked me to give you this. My impression was it's the only reason your lady came to the show. I forgot her name. I hate to keep calling her your lady friend."

"Jewell. Her name is Jewell Hyatt. Dr. Jewell Hyatt. She's a veterinarian from my hometown." Saxon took the envelope. His name was typed on the front.

"Hell's bells! Tell me she's not the Jewell you write all those lovesick songs for but never sing in a show until last night?" The big man clasped his hands between his knees as he leaned forward and stared at Saxon. "Of course she's one and the same. By the way, the guy who ran the sound booth said that song was the biggest hit with your audience. It sent his meter past the hot-damn zone."

"Yeah, well, don't schedule it on the tour. It's personal."

"You've always been stingy with info about your past." He gestured toward the envelope Saxon clutched. "The lady said the letter was from your uncle. How come you never mentioned any family? I'm in the dark even though I've had your back for five years." Donovan slapped him on the back. "So what's in the letter?"

Saxon's lip curled as he dug a finger under the flap and ripped open the envelope. Taking out the single sheet of paper, he scanned the few lines that only requested him to come to the ranch so they could talk. Crushing it into a ball, he dropped it on the couch. "My past is better left buried." Rising, he rubbed his bare chest. "I see the storm's over. I'll grab a shower and coffee. You roust the band. Tell 'em we're off to Nashville for the CMA Music Festival. Plan a lunch stop in West Virginia. After we eat, I'll join the band and we can choose which numbers to do on the tour. I thought we'd mix it up for each venue."

"Smart. Keep it fresh and you all perform better. Oh, I got word from the benefit promoter in LA. They want two songs. You'll be live. Something jazzy to start. Get the audience revved up. Follow that with a tearjerker so people open their wallets and shell out for the charity."

"Okay. Whatever they want." Saxon sidestepped Donovan and padded barefoot down the hall. "Let yourself out," he called over his shoulder.

"You'd do well to sing the love song you did last night no matter how private it is. The one where it's obvious you got your heart broke."

"No! And that's final." Saxon slammed the bathroom door so hard it rocked the bus. Stiff armed, he leaned on the sink, gritting his teeth, telling himself grown men didn't cry. It wasn't until he heard the outer door at the front of the bus bang shut that he was able to emerge from his funk to shower.

He felt somewhat refreshed after donning clean clothes. Going into his bedroom, he decided to strip his bed and put the sheets and pillowcases in to wash. He couldn't bear to sleep there again where Jewell's signature shampoo had left a flowery scent.

After remaking the bed with fresh linens, he cleaned the kitchen of all signs that he'd hosted a guest last night. But as he started loading the dishwasher, he remembered his uncle's letter. It wasn't anything he'd want any band members to see, and they ran in and out of his coach at will.

Hurrying into the living area, he saw that the letter was gone. Obviously Donovan had discarded it for him. Cleaning up after him and the band was a duty of his recording label's babysitter. Which pretty much explained Donovan's role. Who else would show up wearing a suit at 7:00 a.m.? Although today he had dispensed with his usual tie.

Saxon sighed and went back to restoring order to his kitchen. Maybe he needed a break from touring more than he thought. He'd requested downtime after LA. His agent hadn't sounded happy when he said he wanted to hide out and write new songs for a month or two. Granted, he hadn't expected Sid to be overjoyed, but neither had he figured he'd get flak from the label owner. His band said they could use downtime, too. Harmony Records counted on him. So did Sid. Which was why Saxon thought they should realize no one lasted if they performed stale music. Fans demanded new songs every year.

He was in the process of tying up a bag with last night's trash to toss out in the theater's garbage bins when his driver knocked loudly and came in.

"Yo, Saxon, Donovan said we need to pull out. Are you riding with the band?"

"Not until after lunch. Can you give me a minute to throw this away?" He hurried to the front of the coach and held up the bag.

"I'll get it," the cheerful young man said. "There are puddles of standing water outside and you don't have your boots on."

"Thanks, Dean. I'm running on slow speed today."

The man grinned. "It's probably due to last night's low barometric pressure."

Saxon doubted that. He thought it was due to Jewell's abrupt departure, but he didn't argue. He went back to the bedroom to get his boots, knowing they'd be where he'd toed out of them in his rush to get Jewell into his bed.

Still at loose ends after Dean returned and both buses got under way, Saxon decided he'd be best served to sit with his guitar, keyboard and music pad and maybe get a head start on writing a new song.

But he sat staring at the blank page for a long time.

All at once he felt the bus jerk, slide, then smooth out again.

"Jeez," Dean groused. "Sorry, Saxon. There are some low spots filled with water on the road. I don't know if you've looked out, but in places, water's running across the freeway. I had to swerve to miss a stalled car. Some people tried driving through that storm, I guess."

Saxon set aside his guitar and went to the railing behind Dean, where he could see the road out the front window. Traffic was heavy. Passing cars threw spray up from their tires. He pictured Jewell driving on this road when it'd been dark.

He knew she was a good driver and had never been bothered by Montana's deep snow. But traffic there wasn't an issue. Worry for her wouldn't let him get back to work. He didn't have a phone number for her, but hers was probably the only veterinary clinic in Snowy Owl Crossing. Sure he wouldn't rest until he at least knew if anyone had heard from her after the storm, he went to his bedroom to make a private call.

A man answered the number he'd gotten for J. Hyatt, veterinarian. "Uh, hello. I'm trying to reach Jewell Hyatt."

"This is Dr. Cooper. I'm covering Dr. Hyatt's calls. May I help you?"

"I'm phoning from Maryland. I… We had a hurricane here and I'm checking to make sure she got home okay."

"Not yet. She called to say her flight was canceled and there's a backlog. She's rebooked but due back in a couple of days. May I take your name and leave her a message?"

The news that the other vet had heard from Jewell unwound the tight knot in Saxon's belly. "Thanks, it's not necessary." He clicked off then because he didn't want any more questions. She'd made it safely back to DC. That gave him peace of mind.

But even afterward all the chords he jotted down sounded like other songs he'd written. And thoughts of Jewell kept interfering. Words came to him about how her hair looked like fire and her skin like snow. Saxon tossed aside his guitar with a thud and scrubbed his hands down his face. He should shave.

"Everything cool back there?" Dean called. "I like listening to you play."

"I'm okay. Just wrestling with a new song."

"Carson's asking if you're ready to stop for lunch. Up ahead is a steak-and-burger place he knows. Donovan says we can get out and stretch and go inside without locals bugging you for autographs."

"If that's what the band wants, it's fine by me. I don't mind talking to fans. Most are respectful. We need them."

"Yeah. Carson says Donovan worked with rock stars too long. Those fans mob an artist."

"I guess we'll see in a few weeks. The Hollywood benefit features crossover hits as well as country."

"Hey, there's the steak house. I hope it's open. This dinky town looks sleepy or dead."

Saxon stood again and peered out as Dean parked. He could see from one end of the street to the other. The businesses were small and built of weathered wood. As he put on his cowboy hat and swung down out of the bus, he was reminded acutely of Snowy Owl Crossing. Surprisingly, he felt a wave of nostalgia but was abruptly jerked back to the present by his rowdy band members trooping inside the eatery.

Donovan engineered seating so that tables where the band sat acted as a buffer to the back booth he chose for himself and Saxon.

Two waitresses emerged from the kitchen, bringing menus and trays of water glasses to the noisy men. The woman who served Donovan and Saxon smiled and winked at Saxon. "Saw you on TV at the last country music awards. Bought some of your songs for our jukebox." She pointed to the opposite end of the room. "Willie Nelson's been here. Reba, too. They gave us autographed photos we framed and put on the wall. Would be right honored to add you," she drawled.

Donovan sighed and adjusted his tie, but Saxon nodded and smiled. "I'm sure we can scare up a photo I can sign." He passed back the menu. "I smelled burgers when I walked in. That's what I'll have, with a large order of fries."

The others ordered, too, and as soon as the women left, Donovan took a wrinkled paper from his suit pocket. Scowling, he set it in front of Saxon. "Why don't Harmon or Andrews know you have family in Montana?"

Saxon stiffened. Fred Harmon was the owner of his label company, and Sid Andrews had been his agent/manager from the get-go. Saxon snatched the paper, wadded it up and shoved it in his shirt pocket. “What does it matter?”

“You have relatives we don’t know about anxious to see you in person, you bet your butt it’s the label’s business.”

“It’s nobody’s business but mine.” Saxon mustered a thin smile for the waitress who slid a sizzling steak in front of Donovan and a fat burger in front of him.

Donovan waited to speak again until the men at the adjacent tables were served and the waitresses had left. “How old is this uncle? Why can’t he phone you? Is he dying?”

That last question hit Saxon like a barreling freight train. Had Jewell said Leland was sick? “I don’t know.” Squirting ketchup near his fries, Saxon watched Donovan slice his steak. “He’s my dad’s older brother. When my folks died, he was named my guardian. We had a rocky relationship. He thought I should be a rancher, not a singer. This is the first I’ve heard from him since I moved to Nashville.” Saxon pushed a fry through the ketchup, then shoved it in his mouth and picked up his burger. “Can we not discuss this?”

“I knew the redhead who brought the letter spelled trouble the minute you asked to see her backstage. You never invite women to your bus. Now she’s gone and you’re acting weird. I work for Fred. He’s invested a bundle in you. It’s my job to keep you from going off the rails.”

Half choking, Saxon had to take a drink of water. “I earn my keep at the label. As for Jewell, leave her out of it. She had business in DC, so my uncle asked her to deliver his letter."

"I admit you earn your keep. The question is, did you hear from your long-lost uncle because he's suddenly broke and sees you as a potential cash cow?"

"You read his letter. He doesn't say why he wants to see me." Saxon stabbed another French fry in the pool of ketchup.

"While we're in Austin or San Antonio, I'll put out feelers. You know, to see if the old guy's in debt or shopping for a loan."

"No!" Saxon wiped his hands on his napkin, tossed it down on his plate and got up. "Stay out of it, and that goes for Sid and Fred, as well. I get wind of anyone poking around Snowy Owl Crossing, I'll find a new label." He stormed out, aware that his band members had stopped talking and gaped after him.

He got back on his bus, scribbled his name on a photo and took it back in to the waitress. He rarely flew off the handle, and so he was sure band members who'd been with him the longest would be curious. He had to decide how much to tell them. For all Donovan's faults, he didn't gossip. So the guys wouldn't be privy to details about his uncle's letter unless he shared them. However, they'd all seen Jewell, and most knew he'd taken her to his bus. If he said nothing, the guys would speculate that his tussle with Donovan most likely had to do with her. *Damn!*

Back in the bus he paced. Was his uncle sick? Did he need money? When he was growing up, his parents had never even mentioned his uncle. So he'd been in shock to learn someone he'd never met had been named his guardian. He actually didn't know much about his parents' families, period. Maybe he should be the one asking questions. But ask who? Not his uncle. They hadn't spoken since he left home. Jewell? She'd brought his uncle's letter but had claimed she had no idea what Leland wanted. He had no reason to doubt her.

IT WAS LATE afternoon three days after the hurricane when Jewell finally caught a flight out of DC that eventually got her to Billings. Still feeling off-kilter, she would have spent the night in a hotel and driven home in the morning, but she was anxious to get there. She collected her pickup from the long-term lot, grateful the sun would be setting behind her on the drive.

After connecting her cell to the hands-free device, she phoned Pete Cooper, her fill-in at the vet clinic. "Hey, Pete, it's Jewell," she said when he answered. "I'm heading home as we speak. Thanks for taking my calls. I'll pop a check in the mail tomorrow. Did anything come in that I need to handle tomorrow?"

"Not really. Tawana called. The Artsy Ladies plan to meet for a late lunch at the café Monday at one o'clock. She said it's important. I left you a note."

"Ugh! They're probably in a tizzy over the fact I wasn't able to secure an owl refuge. I'm afraid everyone's getting tired of working so hard to earn money at our Thanksgiving bazaars. Be sure to mark your calendar so you and your wife can come again this year. We need all the support we can get."

"Lois loves doing our Christmas shopping there. Hey,

I left a couple of other messages on your desk. The secretary for the Wild Horse Stampede gave me dates and times they need you as the on-duty vet over the Fourth. And a man called but didn't leave a name. He said he'd seen you back east."

Jewell's bruised heart leaped. Had Saxon looked up her number and phoned?

"All the guy said was that he was calling from Maryland. He mentioned the storm and said he wanted to make sure you'd driven through it okay."

Her heart calmed. "It was probably the owner of the horse farm where I had sperm shipped to Mark Watson. He and his wife were nice folks."

"Ah, speaking of the semen straws, Mark got the package. He'll refrigerate it until you can go plug it into his mare." Pete laughed. "Better you than me. I hate artificially inseminating any animal."

"There are jobs I like better. If that's all, Pete, I'll let you get back to doing whatever you were doing before I phoned."

"It's okay. I'm cleaning cages at my clinic." They shared a laugh, then said goodbye.

It was full darkness by the time Jewell turned down the lane to her ranch. Just seeing the buildings fanned out in front of her headlights sent warmth trickling through her. Travel was exhausting. Home spelled comfort.

She stopped outside the garage connecting her house to the barn, which now served as her clinic. All at once she noticed her headlights illuminated an animal cowering behind hydrangea bushes her mom had coaxed to life in the harsh Montana weather. Afraid it might be an injured wolf, Jewell squinted to better see before opening her garage. She had a tranquilizer gun in the barn, but Pete hadn't left an outside light on there. The animal slowly crawled out from under the bush and she saw it was a puppy.

She still left her pickup with care. It could have rabies. But the nearer she got, the more clearly she saw it was nothing but a poor bedraggled, half-starved spaniel. Sinking to one knee, she held out a hand. "Here, boy. I won't hurt you. I don't see a collar, but maybe you have a chip. First I'll check for injuries. Then we'll get you some food, followed by a bath. I'll bet you'd like to get back to your owner, huh?"

The pup crept toward her on its belly, crying pitifully. She scooped him up and felt him curl against her in a ball. "Heavens, your ribs are showing. Food comes first." Cradling him carefully, she hurried to open her clinic. Once the lights were on, she could better see his matted brown-and-white fur.

She carried him into an exam room that in her parents' day had been a horse stall and drew a bowl of water. He lapped it down, his big dark eyes showing his gratitude. She stocked all types of animal supplies and at the moment didn't have other boarders except a goat who'd had surgery before her trip. She didn't hear him, so Pete had probably discharged him.

Not wanting the hungry dog to eat too fast, she measured out a short cup of puppy chow. He gobbled it up but sank down without begging for more. "You have manners. Clearly you're someone's pet." Jewell fondled his ears, which would be silky after a bath. She checked for signs of trauma. All she found were cuts on the pads of his feet. "It appears you've been out running around awhile. Warm soap and water will do wonders, but it'll sting these paws. I have salve for after your bath." She continued to talk because he seemed to like hearing her voice. And ministering to him let her forget the disappointment caused partly by her failure to gain a refuge for the snowy owls and also her lingering sadness for having slept with Saxon when nothing had changed between them. However, the weariness she'd battled earlier fled in the face of caring for the puppy.

"There, well, don't you look handsome," she said after bathing him and toweling dry his curly coat. "I'd say you're a springer spaniel. That explains why you're easygoing and affectionate." She scanned him for a chip and was concerned when she didn't find one. He licked her chin and wagged his tail, then stared longingly at the empty bowl still sitting on the floor.

"That's plain enough. You're so cute I'm going to take you to my house. I still need to retrieve my suitcase and unpack, but I'll feed you in the kitchen." She picked him up along with the bowl and kibble. Going out, she doused the clinic lights and unlocked her house.

She didn't own a dog bed. Long ago she'd learned she couldn't keep every stray dog or cat that landed on her doorstep. But she did have a soft throw rug. And this pup was so cuddly she might buy a dog bed if she didn't turn up his owner.

There was no sense naming him until she knew. Attaching a name was like attaching your heart. When she measured out more food and he nudged her fingers with his tongue and gave a happy bark, she experienced a tug in her chest. Heaven knew since walking away from Saxon for the second time, her heart ached. On the drive home she'd dreaded coming into a dark, empty house. The dog changed all that and made homecoming a little better.

It wasn't long after she brought in her suitcase that the dog seemed ready to settle for the night. And so was she. He curled right up on the rug she placed by her bed. His soft, whiffling snore soon let her sleep.

SOMETHING BLOWING LIGHTLY in her ear partially woke Jewell. She cracked one eye, saw only gray light and shut it again. More insistent wet kisses nuzzled her cheek. "Stop it, Saxon." She batted her face with one hand. Then her morning brain connected with what she'd said and she bolted straight up in bed. Blinking, she saw dark puppy eyes gazing adoringly at her. Jewell laughed and her pounding heart fell into normal rhythm. "You stinker. You made me think you'd spend the night on the rug. In fact, you made yourself at home on my bed."

The pup yawned and licked her nose with a happy little yip.

"Okay, I'm awake. Breakfast time. Then you have to go into one of my holding cages in the clinic. I'll take your picture, make a flyer and distribute it around town."

The minute she looked out the window, it was plain

her first workday home had opened with a gorgeous sunrise.

Jewell hummed as she showered. She ate, fed the pup and made a mental list of what she had to do today. In the course of unpacking last night she'd found the business card of Saxon's agent. Handing it off to Leland would be her first task after she printed up a stack of flyers.

Two hours later, driving along the lane to Leland's house, she saw he had two men tilling his fields. Her breath caught. Had he sold his ranch?

"Hi, Leland," she said, making herself sound more cheerful than she felt when the old guy answered her knock and stepped out on his porch. "What's with your fields?"

"I leased a section to Eddie Four Bear and Aaron Younger. My Realtor says ranches aren't selling. This way I have lease money coming in and the fields look productive. I assume my nephew didn't return with you."

"No." Jewell made a face. "My flight was delayed a few days due to a hurricane. I came to give you a card for Saxon's agent. He's off on a tour. I left your letter with one of his staff. I'm afraid Saxon's not coming here," she said as gently as possible. "If you need anything, call me, please."

The old fellow sighed. "I knew it was a long shot. Thanks for the card," he said and turned away. "I really need to see him. He and I have to talk."

Jewell chewed the inside of her cheek. Was his skin

more sallow than before she'd left? It must be her imagination, or the lighting. She hadn't been gone that long.

After saying goodbye, she spent the morning tacking up flyers about the pup. No one she spoke to had heard anyone say they'd lost a pet.

ALL WEEKEND SHE was kept busy with calls from clients, and she hadn't found time to phone her friends. But on Monday, Jewell left a ranch and drove to town for her lunch with the Artsy Ladies. Running a bit late, she rushed into the Snowy Owl Café at ten after one.

Becky, a high school girl who helped Doreen Mercer after school and during summers, greeted Jewell. "The other ladies are at that back table. They've ordered. What can I get for you?"

"Tuna sandwich. And iced tea. Thanks, Becky."

"Hey, there's Jewell," Tawana announced. "Glad you could make it. You were away extra time and then so tied up you've missed all our news."

Jewell pulled out a chair and stared expectantly at her friends. "I've been working but was also afraid you'd hammer me for not getting the owl refuge."

"Oh, that. We've got bigger news," Shelley, their resident ceramic potter, said around a gulp of iced tea.

Lila leaned toward Jewell. "You missed hearing how Rory went out to the mine, fell down a shaft and broke his arm. He's upstairs now still sporting a cast. But I have good news, too." She displayed her left hand for Jewell to see a sparkling diamond.

Jewell shrieked. "You and Seth are engaged? What?

How? When's the wedding? And another mine accident? This is too much to take in. Is Rory okay?"

"He's lucky but bummed because he can't play baseball the rest of the summer. Seth saved his life. As for our wedding..." Lila named a date three weeks out. "Myra's mom's making bridesmaids' dresses like she did for Myra. Yours, too. I bought my dress. It's seafoam green. Bridesmaids wear jade. We'll be married at the Owl's Nest. Of course, Mom insists on catering the reception."

Jewell gaped. "Whoa. Tell me more about the mine incident."

Myra Maxwell waved a hand. "Wait. Right before you got here, I told everyone Zeke and I just yesterday found out I'm pregnant with twins," she blurted. "Already I feel lumpy. I may not be in Lila's wedding. Maybe I'll cut and serve the cake."

"Rubbish," Lila broke in. "You'll be in the ceremony."

"Two babies?" Jewell jumped up and rounded the table to hug Myra. "How great is that news? I knew you guys wanted children ASAP."

"I was aware I was pregnant for some weeks. But we didn't want to tell anyone until we were sure all was well. Lila, Rory and Seth happened to be in the ER when I had my first ultrasound. But my OB only just heard two heartbeats. We're over the moon."

"So double congratulations. For the record...you don't look lumpy. Gosh, I feel like I've missed months instead of days."

"Tawana has news, too," Lila said.

"Don't tell me you're marrying Hunter."

"Nothing that drastic." Across the table, Tawana bent and came up holding a large picture frame. "But he is moving here."

Jewell saw it was a rodeo scene painted on tooled leather. "Did you make that? Are you branching out from beaded vests and belts? That's gorgeous. I'd commission something like it for my clinic office."

"Hunter did this. He's sorry the storm hit so you guys couldn't connect while you were back east. The best news is he has his final prosthetic leg and can travel here for Seth and Lila's wedding. His craft work looks promising as a new profession. It should sell well at the bazaar. He said he's painted several pictures."

"Each must take hours. I'm sure he can sell them," Jewell said. "Too bad he won't want his earnings to go into our Artsy Ladies' save-the-owl kitty."

"He does," Tawana assured as she set the painting down. "But none of this is why I called this meeting." She motioned everyone closer. "I had a brainstorm after talking to Hunter. Something I believe will make us enough money to buy Leland's ranch. If you agree, we can keep the forest and sell the house and fields on contract to Eddie Four Bear. But…" she chewed her lip "… Jewell, my idea needs your approval."

"Mine? Now I'm really curious. So spill," she said, and the others chorused their agreement. Jewell retook her seat, but they were all forced to wait impatiently as Becky delivered their food. She'd barely left when all eyes pinned Tawana again.

"Hurry up," Mindy said. "I have a client due at my salon at two o'clock."

"All right. Listen up. For weeks the country music station I listen to in my office has advertised a big benefit concert in LA at the end of this month. I guess none of you heard the ads. Well…one featured star is our very own Saxon Conrad." She beamed at her rapt audience, then added, "Think how much we'd rake in if he detoured to give a benefit here and we earmarked all monies above costs to buy Leland's ranch."

Jewell's face fell. She whirled on Lila. "You promised not to tell anyone Leland asked me to attend Saxon's concert in Maryland."

"I didn't. I swear." Lila held up her hands.

Immediately, all stares locked on Tawana swung to Jewell. "You saw Saxon?" the women chimed in excitedly.

"Yes, for Leland," she rushed to say. "Forget the idea. Saxon will never agree."

A hush fell over the table.

"You don't know that," Tawana said. "Honestly, Jewell, what can it hurt to call and ask him? You love the owls more than any of us."

"I c-can't," Jewell said, her voice brittle.

Tawana's gaze shifted to the others. "Who can? Who knows him next best?"

"Not me," Myra ventured. "But I'll give it a go if any of you join me on a call."

Lila pursed her lips. "Jewell, would it hurt you too badly if we can talk him into giving a show here? If not, I'll make a conference call with Myra. Tawana said you told her the Natural Resources Committee might sanction a refuge if we had land. Given how much sweat and tears we've put into this project, seems to me it's worth trying Tawana's suggestion."

"I hate to be a wet blanket, but if Saxon won't come see his only relative after I made plain Leland's not well, he sure as heck won't come for us, or owls. But… I won't stand in your way. Just know he won't come for me," she said, her voice wavering again. "If that's it, can we go back to talking about happier things like Lila and Seth's wedding and Myra's pregnancy?"

It took only a moment for chatter to resume. Jewell let the excitement flow around her. A hole had opened so big in her belly she couldn't eat her sandwich. She did know how much they'd earn if Saxon performed. But he was probably so mad at her for running out on him last week that he'd never want to see her again. If her friends noticed how quiet she'd grown, no one let on.

Lunch ended. Everyone hugged, then went their separate ways.

It wasn't until Jewell was almost home that she realized she'd forgotten to bring up the dog. She actually hoped no one claimed him. She could use his comfort.

Chapter Four

Later that evening Jewell phoned Lila. "I'll be working two days and one night at the stampede. Would Rory like to go with me again this year? You and Seth probably have tons to do to get ready for the wedding. By the way, are his parents coming to the wedding?"

"Yes, and two of his gem-hunter friends. Although he's informed them that talking about their job is off-limits. That's what caused Rory to go into the mine. He overheard one of Seth's buddies rave about someone finding a fortune in rubies, and talk evolved to Montana sapphires. It was dumb luck it rained that day, so I went to fetch Rory from Kemper's house. He said Rory rode his bike out to the mine in search of blue stones. I panicked. At first I blamed Seth. But his cooler head prevailed. He rescued Rory from that shaft. It's only one of the many reasons why I love that man, Jewell."

"I'm happy for you, Lila." And she was, but Jewell envied her friends, too. Perhaps that came from seeing Saxon again. At one time she'd assumed they would marry. Likely Tawana and Hunter would be next. "Uh,

Lila...do you want to ask Rory about the stampede and call me back?"

"Actually, Seth is going to take him. He's never attended a rodeo. I appreciate your offer, but Rory has a serious case of hero worship for his soon-to-be dad."

"I understand."

"You sound hurt. Don't be, Jewell. You're my best friend. We can't let that change."

"I didn't realize I sounded hurt. Sorry, I'm probably still suffering jet lag. Hey, when do I get to see and fit my bridesmaid dress?"

"Myra's mom is bringing her sewing machine and fabric to Myra's house over the holiday weekend. I know you have obligations at the stampede, but I hope you two can work out a time for a fitting. The dress isn't fussy. Seth wanted a splashy wedding. I preferred simple. He said he really just wants me to be happy, so it'll be lower-key than Myra's service was. I'm sorry you weren't here to help choose a pattern or material for the dresses. I hope you're not disappointed."

"Don't fret, Lila. I'll be happy with anything. Surely by now you know I'd be married in jeans and a T-shirt in a horse barn. Hard as it's been on my mom, she finally accepts I'm not a frilly kind of girl."

"Weddings demand a few frills. Frankly, I've always pictured you as a bride who'll wear emerald silk to set off your fiery red hair. I guarantee you won't be married in a barn or on a horse, so there."

Jewell didn't mention that Saxon had suggested a living arrangement of sorts. Instead she cleared her throat. "Enjoy every minute of the process, Lila. I figure Tawana will be next, don't you? She once told me she wants a traditional Native ceremony where she can wear her mother's beaded, fringed white leather wedding dress."

"I remember her saying that," Lila said. "The women in our group are all so different. Seth is amazed I felt comfortable enough to hand over our wedding plans to the Artsy Ladies. It's precisely because we know each other so well." Lila's tone grew serious. "Jewell, are you really okay with Tawana's plan to ask Saxon to give a benefit here? You haven't said what happened when you went to his concert."

"The storm caused it to end early. I can't tell you what it was like seeing him again or I'll start crying. It was bittersweet." Her voice cracked. "But I have to forget him, Lila. As painful as it is to admit, I'll never fit in his world, nor he in mine." She blinked away unwanted tears. "I have to go. If you need help decorating the B and B for the big event, holler. I tie a mean satin bow."

"Thanks. Listen, maybe I shouldn't join Myra when she calls Saxon. I might tell him I think he's a jerk. Honestly, Jewell, if he makes you cry, he doesn't deserve you." Lila paused as the sound of male voices came over the line. "I'm really sorry but Rory and Seth just came in. Gotta run. Are you sure you're okay, though?"

"I'm fine. Go see to your guys." Jewell ended the call and let go of all the tears she'd held in check since leaving Saxon.

The stray pup she had again brought inside for the night whimpered and then hopped up on her bed to lick off her tears. She wrapped him in her arms, not even pretending to make him sleep on his rug. Instead she welcomed how he cuddled against her in her big, lonely bed.

OVER THE NEXT few days she kept busy treating both domestic and work animals. She also handled the insemination of Mark Watson's mare.

The holiday weekend she pulled duty at the stampede during bulldogging, barrel racing and team roping. Jewell loved the hubbub that accompanied the rodeo. Contestants were a warm, friendly lot. And Montana stock providers took excellent care of their animals, which meant her job was easy, allowing her to watch events.

She hated when her last shift ended on Sunday, although she needed to shower and get to Myra's for her dress fitting. They'd invited her to stay for supper, but lately she hadn't been hungry. It wasn't that she'd gorged at the rodeo, either. This year, more than in the past, odors from food vendors mingling with barnyard scents permeated the air throughout the grounds—and she found the smell nauseating.

She told rodeo friends goodbye and dashed home. She didn't plan to stay late at Myra's ranch, the Flying Owl, because ever since returning from DC, she'd felt dragged out. The good thing about tonight's fitting was that Mrs. Odell said she still had her size from when she'd sewn Myra's bridesmaid dresses. Tonight was a matter of fitting the new dress.

Jewell debated taking the pup. As yet, no one had claimed him. He'd been a model companion the day she drove out to count snowy owls. He'd watched the big birds swoop around but hadn't barked or cowered in fright. So she'd begun taking him on calls to ranches. He trailed so closely at her heels she started calling him Shadow. The name stuck.

After she fed him, she rethought taking him to Myra's out of deference for her friend's pet mini pig. Orion, the pig, would be in a tizzy around a dog. That wouldn't be fair.

She backed out of her lane and drove west toward Myra and Zeke's ranch. After only a few minutes she slowed to admire the dazzling evening Montana sky. Rows of lacy vanilla clouds streaked a mango-colored sunset that skimmed the mountaintops. She wondered if Tennessee had skies to compare. Aack! Hadn't she sworn to Lila that she had to forget Saxon? The way he kept popping into her head at odd times, like now, she obviously wasn't succeeding. And she needed to prepare for Myra to mention him. After all, she and Lila intended to phone and ask him to give a charity benefit for the snowy owls. Of course, he wouldn't.

On reaching the ranch, she parked and went to the door.

Myra greeted her wearing sweatpants and a loose-fitting shirt that made her look more pregnant than when Jewell had seen her at the café.

"Excuse me being so casual," Myra said, ushering Jewell inside. "My OB has me wearing a baby girdle while I'm working around the ranch. She claims it relieves back strain. But by the time I finish the few chores Zeke lets me do, I'm ready to let my stomach pooch."

"Maybe you should forgo doing ranch work until after you have the babies. Hey, I see you have new doll-houses for the bazaar. Stay in and build more. Let Zeke handle outside chores."

"Exactly what I told her," he said, coming up behind his wife to rub her shoulders.

Myra made a face at him but then brushed a kiss over his knuckles. The intimacy left Jewell coveting what they had. To hide the sting, she sniffed the air. "I smell food, but I also hear your mom sewing away in the back bedroom. Is there time to fit my dress before suppertime?"

"Zeke bought a smoker a few weeks ago. He's fix-ing ribs outside so we don't heat up the house. That's something else about pregnancy—it's playing havoc with my body's thermostat. I used to toss around hay bales and never sweat. Now the slightest exertion and it pours off me. The doctor says it's normal." She heaved a big sigh. "But you asked about the dresses. Zeke, is there time for Jewell to try hers on?"

"Sure, babe. I thought we'd eat on the screened porch. While you ladies inspect the sewing, I'll go set the table."

"I'll help." Myra linked their hands. "Jewell doesn't need me. I still may opt out of being in the wedding. So Lila's photos won't look like she has one bridesmaid wearing a tent."

"Lila won't care," Jewell protested. "She and Seth would rather have you in their wedding."

"That's what I told her," Zeke said.

"Myra, if your situations were reversed, you'd say

having friends share in a bride's big day is more important than photographs."

"Maybe. Zeke, I'll let you set the table and I'll go get Jewell's opinion on the shapeless dress Mom sewed for me."

Jewell hooked her arm through Myra's and they ambled into the bedroom.

Mrs. Odell stopped sewing and smiled. "Jewell, how nice to see you again. Your dress is hanging on the door. Unless it needs other adjustments, I only have to mark the hem."

Jewell studied the sleeveless sheath. "I told Lila I'm not big on fancy dresses, but that silk is beautiful."

"Mom, where's my circus tent?"

"Myra, it's no such thing." Her mother rolled her eyes. "I said a pair of back darts will give it some form, but you refuse to let me show you."

"Well, Zeke says I should be a bridesmaid. Jewell, too. You can change in the bathroom," she told Jewell. "I'll slip my dress on and let Mom pin some darts so we can see how I look next to you."

"You'll glow like an expectant mother should," Jewell insisted as she took her dress and disappeared into the adjoining bath.

A few minutes later she stepped out and saw Myra's mom pinning Myra's dress. "You may have to do that to mine, too, Mrs. O. It feels loose."

The older woman motioned Jewell to a table where a pincushion sat. "You're right. You've trimmed down since I made your last dress."

"Oh, right! Just what I didn't need to hear," Myra grumped.

Jewell eyed her friend critically. "Has pregnancy affected your brain? You're two inches taller than me. Your legs are longer by far. And that color matches your eyes. Frankly, I can't see any of the weight you claim to have gained. Anyway, no one will notice your tummy if we carry bouquets."

Myra swiveled side to side in front of a full-length mirror. "We will have flowers. Lila put Seth in charge of ordering them. I told her she's nuts, but she's gaga over a rosebush he bought her. Now she considers him the world's authority on flowers. Oh, listen to me. Hormones have made me bitchy."

Jewell grinned. "We all have our moments. Yesterday Vic Jones accused me of being snarky. He rousted me at dawn to check three sick heifers. Driving in, I saw bitterweed blooming along the fence where he grazes cattle, so I called him an idiot. Honestly, he should've known why his cows were sick."

Myra stopped in the middle of slipping out of her dress. "Bitterweed. I haven't heard of any in the area recently. I'll check our grazing sites tomorrow. Did Vic say he'd spray?"

"No, but I'm sure he will. I embarrassed him. I shouldn't have come down so hard on him, but I haven't slept well since I got back from my trip."

"Oh? Any particular reason?" Myra asked after pulling on her sweats.

Jewell hung up her dress and thanked Myra's mom. She buttoned her jeans before answering. "I took in a stray pup the night I got back. I placed a rug next to my bed, but he prefers company. He's a bit of a bed hog."

"A puppy you aren't adopting out? That's a first."

"Um, his owner may call. I tacked up flyers. He's such a sweet dog."

"He must be. Are you sure you're okay, Jewell? You've always worked tirelessly finding homes for strays. Were you more rattled by the committee's refusal to set up an owl refuge than you let on? I'm not alone in thinking you're out of sorts. Tawana said the same when she came to fit her dress."

Zeke called through the bedroom door that supper was ready. Myra opened the door, and Mrs. Odell shut off her sewing machine. That saved Jewell from manufacturing a response. She didn't feel her old self. To get her mojo back, she just needed to forget Saxon.

The others went to wash at the kitchen sink. Jewell stepped over to Orion's pen. Someone had fed him lettuce and celery. She talked to him like she talked to Shadow and bent to rub his soft piggy ears. He closed his eyes and moved his head against her hand. "Orion looks good," she said before taking her turn at the sink. "I remember he used to love going outside to dig in the dirt. I suppose since the episode where an owl almost made off with him, you've curtailed his outings."

"We still take him out thanks to my clever husband." Myra led the way to the porch. "Zeke bought a big wire kennel and cut out the bottom. Put him inside, and Orion can dig to his heart's content. It's the equivalent of his own screened room."

"That's so smart." Jewell stood aside to let Myra take

her seat at the round patio table. Leaving the chair next to Myra for Zeke, Jewell pulled out one on the other side of Mrs. Odell.

Myra passed a bowl of green salad but spared a moment to bestow a loving smile on her hubby, who came in bearing a platter of sizzling short ribs and foil-wrapped objects Jewell assumed were baked potatoes and corn on the cob. Everything looked delicious, but she recoiled from the barbecue odor wafting off the meat. She took a tongful of salad and set the bowl down. Since Zeke extended the platter, she chose the smallest potato, skipped the corn and cut off one rib before deferring to Mrs. Odell.

"Goodness," the woman exclaimed. "If that's all you eat, Jewell, it's no wonder I'm having to take in your dress. Surely, as slender as you are, you're not dieting."

Jewell hated that all eyes turned to her. "I'm not dieting. Myra can tell you I usually eat hearty. Maybe my recent travels disrupted my appetite."

"You blamed travel for messing up your sleep." Myra glanced up from slathering butter on her corn. "At least you're not pregnant. Insomnia and nausea are what sent me to see a doctor." She grinned at Zeke. "My doctor homed right in on my problem. You'd have thought with all of my experience handling pregnant cows, it might've crossed my mind. It didn't, even though we never used anything to prevent pregnancy."

"Myra," Zeke said. "TMI."

Jewell noticed his face had turned red. And Myra's mom looked up from her plate. "You've lost me, Zeke.

You military guys have acronyms for everything. I have to stop Eric frequently and demand he speak English."

"*TMI* isn't militaryspeak, Mom," Myra said. "It stands for *too much information*. And I think it's time to change the subject."

"Yes," the older woman said. "Zeke, with you and your brother both living in Montana, will your folks move here? Especially now that they'll have grandchildren?"

"You'll have to ask them. They hated Boston winters. That's what drove them to the Caribbean."

"Every time your mom calls, she asks about the snowy owls," Myra put in. "She loved the photos you sent her last Christmas."

"Speaking of owls, considering how warm it is, I was surprised to see three hunting yesterday in my newly tilled field. All had pink leg bands." Zeke aimed his statement at Jewell.

"A few returned early. I believe it's because mice and voles are plentiful and our summers aren't outrageously hot. I've seen birds nesting on rocky outcrops, too."

"All the more reason we need to guarantee them a safe refuge," Myra said.

Mrs. Odell nodded. "It's a shame you didn't make headway with the government, Jewell. Would it help if you ladies sent them petitions filled with resident signatures?"

Jewell shook her head. "The committee was receptive, but they have strict rules. They suggested we hook up with established birders who may have deep pockets. I plan to contact Audubon and other wildlife-defender organizations. I've not had time. Hopefully, I can do that between now and Lila and Seth's wedding."

"Have you gone as a group to ask Leland Conrad to donate his forest?" Myra's mother glanced first at her, then at Jewell.

"Mother, he's listed his ranch to sell as a package. His Realtor says the only way to get the forest is to buy the whole ranch. And he wants a pretty penny. Fair, but way more than we've earned at our bazaars."

Zeke licked sauce off his fingers. "Jewell, what might interest other birders to invest in our refuge?"

She shrugged. "Other than saving a beautiful species and it being what they do, I'm not sure. I've always envisioned signs showing the Artsy Ladies donated our refuge. I suppose we could give another group top billing when we post our sanctuary."

Mrs. Odell picked up a rib. "With all the time, energy and money you six women have invested, it'd be a shame to share the spotlight with some Johnny-come-latelies who live elsewhere."

Myra darted Jewell a veiled glance. "Exactly Tawana's point in us asking Saxon Conrad to give a benefit concert here. I know you say he'll refuse, Jewell. But we'll never know unless we try."

Jewell crushed her napkin into a ball and dropped it on the plate from which she'd taken scant few bites.

Zeke cast a troubled peek between her and his wife. "Jewell, I don't pretend to know what the problem is between you, Leland and his singing-sensation nephew. It's cool knowing Saxon Conrad grew up here. His songs were favorites with the troops I served with. If you or Leland have a contact number, where's the harm in having Lila and Myra call him?"

"I don't have his number. I gave Leland a business card for Saxon's agent. Feel free to ask him for it. You know, guys, I appreciate you inviting me to supper, but I worked the rodeo all weekend, plus got up early to treat Vic's sick cows. Would you mind terribly if I take off?"

"You'll miss out on Mom's fresh peach pie," Myra said.

Jewell pushed back from the table. "Honestly, I can't eat another bite."

Myra struggled to get up out of her chair. "I'll walk you out."

"There's no need." Jewell placed a hand on Myra's arm. "You haven't finished eating." She paused by Myra's mom. "Mrs. O., will I need another fitting before the wedding?"

"Not unless you lose more weight. Zeke's mother and I will see the dresses get to the Owl's Nest at least two hours before the ceremony. You can go straight there. I'll have needle and thread for any last-minute nips and tucks."

"Thanks." Jewell bent to hug Myra before walking to the door that led into the house. "Wait. No one said who I owe for the material. And we each should pay for your time, too," she added to Myra's mother.

Mrs. Odell objected. "I love to sew. Plus it gives me an excuse to visit Myra. In fact, keep me in mind for when you tie the knot, Jewell."

Jewell laughed hollowly. "Don't hold your breath.

If ever that day comes, you'll be off and retired somewhere, leaving your son to run your ranch."

"It's plain you don't know my husband. *Retirement* isn't in his vocabulary."

"It's hard to give up ranching when it gets in the blood," Myra agreed. "As for the fabric, Jewell, Tawana put it on her credit card, so pay her. If I recall, we had this same discussion when Mom made dresses for our wedding." She gestured at Zeke, who kept eating but had tuned out of the dress discussion.

"Okay. But as good as you are at making fine dresses, you should hang out your shingle to sew wedding gowns and bridesmaid dresses as a business."

The older woman blushed. "For me it's a labor of love. I'm so happy that Myra has made so many wonderful friends in her grandparents' community."

Jewell pushed open the kitchen door. "Thanks again. I guess next time I see you all will be the start of August at Lila and Seth's wedding."

"Earlier. Lila wants help decorating the B and B. And we need to finalize terms before Lila and I try to reach Saxon. We should have two possible dates, a site, and how far and wide we're willing to advertise. Since I volunteered to call him, I checked him out online. I didn't realize he was such a superstar. You may be right, Jewell—he'll probably brush us off."

Jewell said, "Yes," from inside the kitchen but realized her words might not have reached her friends, since the door slammed shut on her heels. It wasn't worth repeating. How many times could she warn that Saxon would say no?

Once in her pickup, she battled a sick feeling that her friends weren't going to let her opt out of their scheme to book Saxon. Although the plan had merit, because of the way she left him in Maryland, she knew there wasn't a snowball's chance in hell he'd agree.

Fifteen minutes later she parked in her garage and headed for the house. She opened the door and fancied she heard Saxon talking. She grabbed the doorknob to fend off dizziness sweeping over her. It took a few seconds to get that his voice was coming from her answering machine. She had extensions in the clinic and house so she wouldn't miss an emergency call. But what was he saying? Her ears buzzed.

Shadow barked at the sound. His tail swept back and forth across the tile floor.

Jewell steadied herself on the counter, but all she caught was Saxon saying, "Either you're ignoring me, or you're out on a call. Like I said, I'm in San Antonio. Tomorrow we're off to Luckenbach. According to Donovan, phone service from here to there is spotty. Considering how you ran out on me, I wouldn't ask for your help. But I don't want the owner of my recording label to have lawyers contact Uncle Leland. I know you said you don't know why he wants to see me. But I don't know anyone else who might find out. Fred Harmon believes Leland plans to squeeze me for money. I don't know. You can call me or leave a message. Or I'll phone again from some other stop. I have concerts in a different town every night between here and LA."

The machine crackled and stopped. A light began to blink and Shadow loped over to stand on his hind legs and paw at Jewell's knees. She dropped down on shaking legs and hugged his furry body close until she was able to feel like she could stand again without fainting.

She deliberately filled Shadow's water bowl and put kibble in his empty dish before she collected the wherewithal to play back Saxon's entire message.

He sounded so close it sent prickles up her spine. By concentrating, she managed to get the gist of his call. Leland's note to him had been short on content. But his uncle asked to see Saxon in the flesh. Saxon even said he'd called Leland's house but either Leland or someone else hung up without speaking. That was why Saxon's recording company figured Leland was after money. It sounded as if Saxon wanted her to do his dirty work and press Leland as to why he sent the letter.

She didn't want to get in the middle of it. Maybe Leland had never wanted a family. Maybe he felt like a fish out of water trying to step in and be a dad. As a kid, she'd seen only Saxon's side. Age and distance brought a willingness to consider there could be legitimate reasons for Leland to want to see his nephew.

Darn it all, if Saxon and his boss needed answers so badly while he was running around the country, he should swing through Montana and see for himself.

One thing, though, Saxon had left his cell number. She scribbled it on a pad lying next to the machine. She ripped off the sheet and dropped it in her junk drawer. Maybe she'd pass on Saxon's private number to her friends, but maybe not.

Still a tad irritated at his thinking she'd be his snoop, Jewell stalked off to bed. She didn't fall asleep. Either

Saxon's call or what little she'd eaten tonight gave her indigestion.

Even Shadow issued a series of impatient huffs before he settled down. Beads of sweat formed on her forehead, and soon Jewell kicked off her covers. Long after the dog slept, she watched the clock's minute hand creep along. Each time she nodded off, she jerked awake sure she was hearing Saxon's voice—silly, of course.

She got up and went to the kitchen for antacids and a glass of water. While there, she erased his message, something she'd been reluctant to do earlier.

The message might be gone, but the memory of hearing his voice lingered. And a goal she'd set when she sneaked out of his bus in the aftermath of their romp in his bed—to go home and forget him—continued to hover out of reach.

Chapter Five

Stepping out of his bus as the sun was sinking in the sky, Saxon wove through a crowd seeking his autograph before the evening show in Luckenbach. He imagined they were the sons and daughters of once-avid fans of Willie and Waylon and the song they'd recorded in the '70s that put this rural Texas town on the map.

Donovan tried to hurry him along, saying they needed to check the setup since neither Saxon nor his band had performed here before. Saxon shrugged him off. He felt he owed his fans. When they finally made it into the building, Donovan pulled him aside.

"You look grim." Saxon clicked his ballpoint closed and stored it in his shirt pocket. "Are there problems with the concert arrangements?"

"Nope. You said you'd handle finding out what your uncle wants. Fred expected me to report back."

"I told you to leave it to me. Sid and Fred know I requested a month off after the benefit in LA. If I haven't learned anything by then, I may fly to Montana to see what the hell's going on."

"Fred's not keen on giving you that much downtime."

"Tough. It takes downtime to write new material."

"Even so, there's still the matter of the old guy insisting on seeing you. What if he doesn't want to wait until we finish in LA? What if he disrupts this tour?"

"He lives in the back of beyond, Donovan. What exactly do you guys fear he'll do to hurt me?"

"Fred and Sid are afraid the old geezer may talk to tabloids if he needs money. He could hurt you and the label."

Saxon snorted. "There's no scandal in my past."

"You need to squeeze the redhead to get you the skinny. Fred's so uptight he has Sid meeting us in LA."

"Jeez…why?"

"Partly over your long-lost relative. And partly to talk you out of taking a break. Your stock is up in the industry. Fred wants you to keep touring. Don't forget who made you a star."

Saxon hooked his thumbs over his belt. "In the seven years since Fred signed me, I've quadrupled his investment. Loyalty should cut both ways."

"Yeah, well, at thirty-one it's easy to flame out. And there are always young guns waiting in the wing."

"Like Corbett Knight? I noticed Fred handed him some early songs I wrote and brought to Harmony. I'm glad Sid is coming to LA. It's time he makes sure future songs I write will be exclusively my intellectual property."

"So this time-out is really about song rights? Sid's worried it has to do with the surprise visit from your lady friend. Listen, he can negotiate rights. But not if you want time off touring to go all lovesick, homesick or cow eyed over some woman from the Montana boondocks."

As he digested Donovan's unsubtle advice, Saxon accepted the guitar Carson stopped to hand him. The instrument, very like the one belonging to Jewell's dad that he'd learned on, sent good memories flashing through his head. After seeing Jewell again—and after holding her and making love with her—maybe he was lovesick and homesick. He certainly hadn't been able to get her out of his mind. Merely hearing her voice give instructions to leave a message on her answering machine had left him yearning. But she hadn't phoned him back. Probably he was stupid to wish for a different outcome from someone who'd twice split up with him.

"I'll think on it," he growled, brushing past Donovan to follow Carson.

ABOUT TWO WEEKS after Jewell fit her bridesmaid dress, the Artsy Ladies arranged to meet at the Owl's Nest to decorate for Lila's wedding.

Jewell debated going. She didn't feel well, but she wasn't unwell enough to see a doctor. She frequently felt fuzzy headed, and she hadn't gotten her appetite back. That was so unlike her, given how hard she worked.

To her knowledge, no one she worked for had the flu. And the weather couldn't be more summery, although there was dust and ragweed around. Her frequent headaches could be allergies. Unless they were caused by worrying about Leland and Saxon. After deciding not to give Saxon's private phone number to his uncle, she changed her mind and headed over to his ranch.

Leland took longer than normal to answer her knock. Jewell thought he sounded short of breath. Instead of inviting her in for coffee, as he sometimes did when she brought warm coffee cake, like today, he thanked her for it and the number. But he said plainly enough that he didn't want to talk to Saxon on the phone. He needed to see him. He also ignored her question as to whether he was ill. And did the same when she discreetly asked why it was so urgent he see Saxon in person.

Her concern remained even after she drove out to check on the owls. From there she inspected a load of cattle going to market. That done, feeling extra weary, she opted to stop at the café for supper.

Lila's mom, Doreen Mercer, called Jewell to the pass-through. "Have you seen Leland recently? He almost always comes for lunch. He hasn't been here this week. I phoned him yesterday and this morning, but he didn't answer."

"I saw him earlier today. I don't keep regular tabs on him, Doreen."

"At least you saw him. I hope he's eating healthy."

"I can't say. I took him a coffee cake and he thanked me."

"I'm probably worrying over nothing," the older woman said. "We've been unusually busy, but I need to find time to go see how he's getting along. He looked gray last time he was in."

"Well, he's not planting fields this year, so he hasn't been out in the sun."

Later, at home, Jewell revisited Doreen's concern for her neighbor. Should she try calling Saxon wherever he was on his tour? Would he care that she and Lila's mom had concerns about his uncle's health? Or was she looking for an excuse to contact him and tell him she hadn't learned why Leland wanted to see him?

She'd gotten over being irritated at Saxon for trying to pawn off a responsibility that was really his. She went so far as to check his tour schedule online. It was quite extensive. And hadn't he indicated he'd call her again? She was wasting entirely too much time on grown men who couldn't seem to settle old wrongs.

What she really needed to do before going out to Lila's to decorate was contact the list of known birder activists. She got right on it, but the calls were discouraging. While all the spokespeople applauded her group's efforts to secure a refuge, all cited a downtrend in contributions as the reason they couldn't help.

Jewell fed Shadow and tended animals in her sick bay before she left her clinic.

The other Artsy Ladies were fashioning peach satin bows when she hurried into the B and B a bit late. "Your color scheme is gorgeous, Lila. Shall I start looping ribbon between newel posts?"

Myra handed her a roll and she set to work. Her escort at the ceremony would be Eric Odell, Myra's younger brother. She liked him, but at his sister's reception he'd ditched her to huddle with other ranchers. Unlike her friends' escorts, Eric hadn't asked her to dance. She had no reason to suspect he'd be more attentive this time. Jeez, she shouldn't feel like a fifth wheel. With the exception of Seth Maxwell's gem-hunting buddies, she'd know everyone. What did it matter if she was an unattached wallflower? Oh, boy, was she feeling sorry for herself. That was so unlike her.

"This renders the B and B useless for a while," Lila announced. "Our pastor chose the dining room to hold our service. I had to stow all of my sewing stuff, so I'm way behind making baby sleep sacks for the Thanksgiving bazaar. Well, I'd stopped earlier to sew satin slipcovers for chairs Seth rented. There's still so much to be done, and time's flying past."

"Are you taking a honeymoon?" Shelley asked.

Lila wrinkled her nose. "Two or three days in Billings. Seth needs to visit his college counselor and book the online classes he needs to complete his teaching certification. My mom's keeping Rory."

"I'll board Ghost," Jewell volunteered, mentioning Rory's dog. "I can run by and feed your horses, too, if you'd like."

"Would you? That would be a huge help. Seth thought maybe one of his buddies who plans to stay at the B and B might do it. But he's not sure any of them know a thing about horses. And they may run up to Canada, anyway."

"Lucky you two finagled a few days away since Seth starts teaching right after Labor Day," Myra said. "Like you said, time's flying. The bazaar will be here before we know it, too. Oh, and, Jewell," she called up the stairs, "Zeke saw a large contingent of snowy owls today. He's afraid it means we're in for an early winter."

"I counted three new nests." Jewell leaned over the top railing. "I'm super bummed because the birding organizations I called to see if they'd partner with us all said no. They claim their budgets are already stretched thin."

As the friends continued to tie bows along the curved staircase, Myra said, "I spent part of two weeks trying to chase down a way to reach Saxon Conrad." She shot Jewell an apologetic glance. "Doreen got his agent's number from Leland. But the agent's secretary referred me to his label company. The woman I spoke with there laughed uproariously and asked if I knew how many people called wanting their artists to perform at charities for lifesaving events. She said saving birds was a first but then didn't give the slightest indication she'd pass along my number."

Mindy descended the stairs and got a new roll of ribbon. "I suppose we sound like nutjobs to people who see birds as pests."

"For sure the women saw me as a pest," Myra grumbled.

Lila's son, Rory, who still wore a cast on his broken arm, spoke up. "Maybe my class can raise money once school starts. I'll ask," he said from the table where he painstakingly folded foil around squares of groom's cake. "All the kids love the owls."

His offer moved Jewell. "That's kind of you, Rory, but your classmates' parents already spend a lot at the bazaar." Feeling guilty, she blurted out a phone number. "That's Saxon's cell number. Sorry I didn't provide it earlier. He left a message on my answering machine. The owner of his label is sure Leland's after money. To tell you the truth, it irked me, and I only just gave Leland the number. It makes no sense to me, but he doesn't want to talk to Saxon on the phone. If they can't even talk, I'm more convinced than ever that Saxon won't give us the time of day."

Everyone fell silent a moment. Finally, Lila shrugged and exclaimed, "Well, what's the old adage…nothing ventured, nothing gained? Say that number again, Jewell. I'll jot it down. Myra, if you drop by the café tomorrow, we can go up to Mom's apartment and try calling him. If he hangs up on us, we can quit worrying how to get out ads between now and Labor Day. That's the date Myra and I chose for the benefit."

"Why not closer to the bazaar?" Jewell dropped the bow she held, and her stomach churned at the possibility such a benefit might materialize next month.

"Our plan is to nab him while he's on the West Coast," Myra said.

Tawana, who worked on the opposite stair railing from Jewell, paused to study her. "There may be an urgency for us to do this quickly, Jewell. I told the others this before you arrived. Wednesday a scout for an independent logging company came into the tribal office asking about an old-growth forest he'd spotted from the air."

"Oh, no!" Jewell had bent to retrieve the bow but sat heavily on the landing and grabbed the railing to steady herself. "Leland's trees?"

"Yes. He asked if the timber belonged to us. I could've sent him to Leland. Instead I ran copies of some old plat maps, which I hope confused him since tribal lands do butt against Leland's property. Our council left an undeveloped swath all the way to the

Canadian border, so the guy could assume we own everything and move on."

"I hope so," Myra said. "We cattle ranchers don't need loggers disrupting our open grazing areas with their noisy chain saws. To say nothing of how barren it'd look if someone cut those beautiful evergreens."

"And the owls would go away." Jewell stood. "We're lucky you were at the tribal office when he came in, Tawana. Although a logging outfit probably wouldn't want to buy Leland's house, barns and farmland, either. So far he's stuck by his Realtor's advice to not divide his holdings. I have no idea if he needs money. But he's had his ranch on the market a year."

Lila spoke from below, where she'd gone to cut more foil for Rory. "If Leland's health is failing, as my Mom believes, he might be persuaded to sell his forest for the right price."

"Jewell, what's your thought? You see him more often than the rest of us," Shelley said as she cleaned up empty ribbon spools.

"Leland's an enigma. He doesn't look well, but I haven't been able to find out if something's wrong. I've no idea why he reached out to Saxon. If he needs money to pay taxes or for some other reason, as Saxon's boss believes, who knows what he's apt to do?" Jewell heaved a sigh.

Tawana looped ribbon around the last newel post. "I know he made a deal for Eddie and Aaron to plant and harvest winter crops at a fifty-fifty split."

Myra descended the stairs yawning and rubbing the small of her back. "I have to go home. I'm lumbering under the weight of two extra bodies. If you all want Lila and me to proceed with asking Saxon to give a benefit here, say aye now."

Shelley, Mindy, Lila and Tawana all chorused aye without hesitation. Jewell was two heartbeats behind the others, but she did mutter, "Aye."

Lila beamed at her. "You're really giving us your blessing?"

"Yes," Jewell said on the tail of a sigh. "How can I not support any attempt to secure the snowies a refuge? Heaven knows I've not been successful. If by some miracle you guys convince Saxon, I'll help with whatever is needed."

A cheer went up from the others. As the work party ended, Lila sent Rory off to bed, and the friends filed out. Some paused under the porch light to wish good luck to the two who'd volunteered to call Saxon.

"Shall we all meet at the café Friday for breakfast?" Lila said. "If Myra and I have luck reaching him, we can divvy up concert chores. If not, it'll be our last gathering before my wedding."

"No, wait," Mindy called from the bottom porch step. "Saturday morning of the wedding, if you all come to my salon, I'll do everyone's hair free of charge."

There were more cheers and a consensus to meet on Friday.

SAXON LEFT THE outdoor stage after he and the band finished their last practice session for the LA charity. He stopped to say hello to another country singer, who asked if he ever sold any songs he wrote. They talked a bit, and then Carson passed by and took his guitar. "Sid's waiting for you out where they've set up chairs in the park."

"Thanks." Saxon told the other singer he'd be in touch and dropped his sunglasses over his eyes before moving into the bright sunlight.

"Hey, good rehearsal," Sid called. "Are you free for lunch?" He slapped Saxon's shoulder.

"Sure. I was going to eat at the hotel."

"I'd prefer a quiet restaurant where we can talk," his agent said.

"Okay. We rolled in late last night. I don't know of any place that fits that bill."

"There's a place in the next block I've heard about. Shall we try to get a table?"

Nodding, Saxon fell in step. He'd seen Sid bluster his way into many an establishment. He did so again today.

"It's beastly hot," the older man groused, shedding his jacket at the table a waiter found for them at the back of the room. "Didn't you roast up on that stage?"

"It was warm. But we don't perform until after sunset tomorrow," Saxon said, opening the menu. He chose a shrimp salad and a light beer. As he waited for Sid to order a pasta dish, Saxon mulled over what he wanted to say to his agent.

He almost changed his mind when Sid ordered a double shot of bourbon. His agent rarely drank except for when they were in tense negotiations.

Sid's liquor came, along with Saxon's beer. "If this meeting is about my uncle, I've gotta say I don't know any more than I did before the tour started."

"Let's eat before we talk." Sid gulped his bourbon.

Saxon spun his beer glass around, grateful when their waiter appeared with bread. He buttered a slice.

Seeming to reconsider talking, Sid leaned close. "What I'm gonna say is on the q.t., Saxon. Based on sales for your latest single, coupled with attendance on this tour, Fred's number crunchers say there's a high probability you'll be nominated for CMA Entertainer of the Year. It'd be best if we make sure your uncle gets lost again so he doesn't make waves."

Saxon choked. "Those awards are fan nominated."

Talk was suspended while the waiter delivered their food.

Spinning his pasta around his fork, Sid grinned. "Yes, but Fred's people know stuff. By the way, according to him, it's a piss-poor time for you to take time off."

Saved from answering by his cell phone chiming, Saxon dragged it out of his pocket and started to silence the ring. Then he saw the incoming call had a Montana prefix. An unexpected pleasure marched up his spine. Assuming Jewell was calling to tell him what his uncle wanted, he put a smile in his voice. "Hello there!"

"Saxon?" A woman he didn't recognize hesitantly breathed his name. *Not Jewell.*

His throat tightened in disappointment. "Yes, but you caught me at lunch. Who is this?"

Two voices blurted, "Myra Maxwell and Lila Jenkins. Soon to be Maxwell also," one speaker added. "We only need a second. Jewell said she told you about the Artsy Ladies' quest to secure a snowy owl refuge. We're raising money for land. Since you're our most talented favorite son, we wonder if you'd come give a charity concert here. On Labor Day if possible. All funds earned above your expenses will go toward a refuge."

Too stunned to find his voice, Saxon mentally seized on the request. He wasn't sure which woman delivered it, but he knew Sid had heard some of the call when he vigorously bobbed his head. Surprised, Saxon managed to say, "That may be doable. Like I said, I'm at lunch. Can I get back with you? Which of you shall I ask for at this number?"

"Lila. We attended part of elementary and high school together. But are you shuffling us off? Whether you say yes or no, we'd like to know today. Labor Day's close, and my wedding is this Saturday. I'll be gone awhile, so if your answer is yes, our group has major work to do to get out the word."

"I will call back. Now I have a question. Does Jewell know about this?"

"Yes."

"Ah, is she on board?" Saxon asked, pinching the bridge of his nose.

"She gave us your number."

"Okay, give me half an hour." He heard the caller say thanks as he hit Disconnect and set his phone on the table.

Sid rubbed his hands together. "We can hype another worthy charitable event to your advantage with fans. While you're there, you can quietly dispense with the stickier issue of your uncle."

"I still need time to write. Sid. When I was up for

Male Vocalist, I was expected to perform something original."

"True. Let's see." Sid punched up a calendar on his cell. "I took the liberty of booking you and the band this weekend at a famous bar in Bakersfield. Merle Haggard, Buck Owens and other country singers got their starts there. And I arranged a show at a club in San Francisco. Fred asked me to book you in several events between now and the CMAs. How much time off are we talking?"

"A month. Maybe I can do it in less. But anything I write, I want the sole copyright." Saxon glanced up as the waiter returned to ask if they needed anything else.

Sid waved the man off. "You win this award, I'll get you your song rights." Sid waited until the server left. "Mind if I ask, what the hell are snowy owls?"

Picking up his phone, Saxon tapped a few buttons and extended a photo. "They're a sight, especially when they hunt. Their wingspan can be three or more feet."

"Do people eat them? Are they like wild turkeys?" Sid downed more pasta.

Saxon clicked off the picture. "No! I remember we were kids when Jewell found a stray one in the area and nursed its broken wing. Her trip east had to do with seeing some government committee about a refuge. The owls may be endangered." He tried to recall what she had said.

"No matter. Send the promo department those photos and a bit of history. Leave out Jewell's name. I'll have Fred have photographers do shots of you there."

Saxon toyed with his salad. "I promised my band a break. I'll do this Montana event alone."

Sid blotted his mouth with his napkin. "Good. Perfect, in fact. I'll get you travel vouchers and a credit card to rent a vehicle."

Saxon broke a piece off his garlic bread. "So you want Dean to drive my bus back to Nashville?"

"That'll work. We can spread the word that you've requested privacy to write new material. That will satisfy fans."

"I doubt you'll be surprised to hear I left hard feelings and unfinished business behind in my old hometown, Sid." Even as he said it, Jewell's pretty face loomed in his thoughts. And he wondered why she hadn't been the one to call him.

"Well, don't rock any boats. Oh, and Donovan has the info on the California side events. He'll handle CD sales. Shouldn't you be calling that woman back?" Sid checked his watch, dropped his napkin and swept up the check. "I'll fill Fred in. Be sure you keep in touch. Entertainer of the Year is a big damned deal."

Saxon knew it was. He picked up his phone, but in the periphery of his mind fear crept in about going home to where he'd hurt and been hurt—to where he'd burned bridges. Jewell might have given his phone number to her friends, but did she want to see him again? Or was her involvement all about the owls?

His stomach balled. He could as easily call Lila back and decline. Yes, he could. But he wouldn't.

He wadded his napkin and set it next to his plate.

The anxious-looking waiter appeared. “Were the meals not to your satisfaction?”

Saxon stood. “They were fine. Business cut short our lunch.”

The man picked up the plates. “The cashier would like your autograph, but she’s too shy to ask.”

Saxon wove past other diners to stop at the register. “I hear you’d like an autograph.”

“Oh, yes. I so love your music,” the young woman gushed. “I have tickets to your performance in the park. All of my friends do.”

“Thanks. We’ll be giving away T-shirts. Be sure to get one.” Saxon smiled and left the restaurant. He did have loyal fans, he mused, and hit Redial on his cell.

Chapter Six

Jewell still wasn't sleeping well. She'd worked hard all week helping a local sheep rancher vaccinate his flock. She'd taken Shadow along. He seemed a natural at herding. The dog was so adept Jewell wondered if he'd lived on a sheep ranch. She'd had him a month and no one had inquired about him.

It was after dark when she got home. She really expected a message from Lila or Myra saying they'd struck out getting Saxon to agree to a concert. She hated feeling dejected at no news. But she was.

AT SIX TEN the next morning she dragged herself into the café for breakfast and spotted her friends at their usual table. Early-rising ranchers filled other spots.

Doreen slapped the bell sitting on the pass-through. Jewell saw Lila jump up and rush to deliver steaming plates.

It wasn't until Jewell was deep into the restaurant that the smell of cooked bacon curdled her stomach. She reached her friends and sat heavily in an empty chair.

"Hey, you look peaked," Tawana said. "What's the matter? Are you sick?"

The other women stopped talking and turned to look at Jewell.

She shook her head. "Doreen burned bacon. For a moment the odor was overwhelming."

Myra laughed and patted her protruding stomach. "Boy, am I thankful to be past the first three months of pregnancy. Before that every cooking smell in the morning had me retching. Now I'm just hungry for everything in sight."

As the other women commiserated, an odd fear raced through Jewell. Letting their talk swirl around her, she racked her brain to recall if she'd missed her July cycle. Her periods weren't like clockwork. And Saxon had used protection, after all.

She pressed a hand to her belly. These flu-like symptoms had occurred with increasing frequency since she'd returned from the trip where foolishly she'd been carried away by old feelings. Really, she'd been weak. No, her brain argued—those feelings for Saxon hadn't changed. But what if other things had?

Lila reappeared and slid into her chair. "Okay, getting together today may not have been my best idea. I forgot there's a ranchers' association meeting at the Grange Hall this morning. The guys always come in for breakfast first. Where were we? Myra, did you tell Jewell that Saxon agreed to come give us a show?"

Jewell's breath stalled as her gaze bounced from one to the other of her friends.

Myra said, "So, Jewell, we'd barely told the others.

We caught Saxon at lunch. He phoned Lila back. To our shock, she didn't even have to talk fast to get him to agree to come. Not his band. They'll be elsewhere. But he's who people pay to see and hear." Myra finished and took a big drink of her milk.

Lila jumped up again. "Mindy, our orders are up. Come help, please. Jewell, what can I have Mom fix for you?" She paused as Mindy headed to the pass-through.

"Uh…nothing," Jewell struggled to say. "You aren't kidding? Saxon really said he'd perform here?"

"Really. He didn't argue or anything. He didn't mention Leland, but maybe you set him to thinking when you took him that letter." Lila moved to let Mindy place plates of pancakes and eggs in front of Tawana, Shelley and Myra. "Come on, Jewell, order a short stack. I can tell our news sent you reeling, but you need to eat."

Their news stunned her, but she was already off-kilter from Myra's offhanded comment about morning sickness. She concentrated on unrolling her silverware from a napkin. "Tell your mom I'll have dry toast and apple juice."

"If you're sure that's all you want, I'll turn in your order and deliver food to Hank Watson's table. While I'm gone, start talking about the best way to advertise the show. Time is short, you know."

All eyes rotated to Jewell.

Tawana waved her fork. "Right before you arrived, we all said how much we like the flyers you tacked up about the dog you found. The letters stood out and the picture was visible at a distance. If you did something similar, maybe showing Saxon with his guitar, we could each take a stack and post them here and in neighboring towns."

"I d-don't have any ph-photos of Saxon, with or without his guitar," Jewell stammered, all the while picturing the T-shirt with his likeness that she'd gotten at his concert. A T-shirt she'd been wearing to bed since coming home.

"Can you snag one off his label's website?" Shelley asked.

"Possibly." Jewell fought down mounting panic. "I gave Leland a business card for Saxon's agent. I could call him. Maybe he'd email me a professional photo."

Lila returned with her own plate in time to hear Jewell. "Is it wise to tell Leland? What if he tries to contact Saxon in advance and it turns Saxon off?"

"Guys, Leland shops in town. Anyway, given how fast rumors travel, he's bound to hear. Plus he's my neighbor. Isn't it better he hear this from me?"

The others shrugged. Finally, Myra said, "You know them both better than any of us. And if the concert nets enough money, someone, probably you, Jewell, has to approach Leland about buying his timber for the refuge." She let the sentence drop since Lila's mom came out of the kitchen, bringing Jewell's breakfast.

"Are you talking about Leland?" Doreen asked. "I saw him yesterday afternoon. I took Rory to get his cast off. Leland was at the clinic to see the new cardiologist who recently joined Dr. Rice's practice."

"Heart doctor?" Jewell crumbled the crust from a slice of toast.

"Yes. He's been seeing someone in another town for

skipped heartbeats. That doctor gave him medication, but his condition hasn't improved. We talked when he stopped at the desk to request records from the other doctor. I'm going to take him heart-healthy lunches for a while. Jewell, could you go by at suppertime with grilled chicken or baked fish? He fries way too much."

Lila stared openmouthed at her mother. "Mom, why would you take on all that extra work? How can you leave the café at lunchtime?"

"He's a nice man who doesn't have family, Lila. Over the years he's spent a lot of money here. I asked if he'd eat at one o'clock instead of noon. He's fine with that."

Lila continued to gape, so Jewell touched Doreen's hand. "I've tried to stop by often to see if he's okay. Now that you've suggested I take him supper, I'll be glad to."

Shelley tapped her knife on her water glass. "Hey, are we going to talk about Leland or figure out our chores for this concert? I have a class coming to my ceramics studio in half an hour." She opened a small notebook and pushed her plate aside. "Someone needs to book the Grange Hall. Mrs. M., can you supply cookies and soft drinks? We'll pay for ingredients…right?" She belatedly included the others.

"Definitely," Tawana said, stacking her plate with Shelley's and Mindy's since she, too, had finished eating.

Jewell checked her watch. "I need to get back to my clinic to check on an older cat I'm boarding after surgery. I'll make flyers, but we need a place and time first."

"I'll list what I need," Doreen said, then left, stopping along the way to pick up plates and patrons' money.

"Since tomorrow's my wedding and then we'll be

away until late Tuesday, I can't see about the Grange Hall. If it's not available, could we set up in the park? Maybe borrow folding chairs from a couple of churches."

"I'll leave here and go see about the hall," Mindy volunteered. "The park is a lot more trouble. What about a sound system? We can't ask Saxon to provide one."

Jewell, who'd eaten a half slice of toast, brushed crumbs off her lips. "The Grange has a sound system. Give me a shout, Mindy, if the hall is free. I'll start on a flyer once a spot's nailed down. Unless I get super busy at the clinic, I can place ads in surrounding newspapers. We'll need them to run next week. That only gives us four weeks to sell tickets."

"Boy, we didn't allow ourselves much time to pull this together," Tawana said. "I'll ask Hunter to go tack up flyers in Wolf Point. He's in limbo waiting for his leather-craft stuff to be delivered."

"Is he staying at Lila's B and B?" Jewell asked.

Tawana blushed bright red. "He…uh…is bunking at my place."

That had everyone but Jewell teasing her. She tried to act happy—for all her friends. First Myra fell in love, married and was now pregnant with twins. Lila was about to be married. And Tawana was clearly on top of the world. *Only a jealous witch wouldn't be ecstatic for them.* She didn't want to be like that, so she swept it from her mind and took money out of her wallet to pay for her breakfast.

"Mindy, what time should we be at your salon tomorrow? Are you sure you want to do everyone's hair?"

"I do. I found the sweetest fake baby roses in peach.

I showed Lila how they'd look braided in our hair. She loved them. Since the wedding is at two, come at ten. I'll serve lattes and biscotti."

"Who'll weave the roses in your hair?" Shelley asked.

Mindy laughed. "I'm good. Don't worry. I practiced on myself."

"After Mindy finishes our hair, we can all go to the Owl's Nest to dress," Lila exclaimed. "Myra's mom and Seth and Zeke's mother will meet us there with the dresses."

Tawana set out her money. "What about Seth? You don't want him to see you in your gown the day of the wedding. That's bad luck."

"My gown is just a cocktail dress. And that's a silly superstition. Apparently, though, Seth believes it. He's taking Rory to Zeke's until guests arrive. Did I tell you Seth bought Rory a new suit? And got them matching ties."

"That's cool. What a great guy." Mindy sighed. "I hope you all left some good men out there for me to find. What about you, Jewell?"

She'd gotten up and was pushing her chair back under the table. "What about me?" she asked with a start.

"I said I hope all of our friends who are suddenly attached to fabulous men left some. Don't you wish that, too?"

"I haven't thought about it one way or the other," Jewell muttered. "Listen, I've gotta dash. I'll see you all in the morning." She left quickly, trying not to picture the fabulous man she'd kicked to the curb not once but twice.

She drove home to check on the cat. The surgery site

looked good, so it was with shaking hands that she sat down with a calendar to count the days since her last period. That sent her from vague fear into high anxiety. But, she still clung to the fact Saxon had used protection.

She grabbed her keys again, loaded Shadow in her pickup and headed to a nearby town she knew had a twenty-four-hour pharmacy—a store where she could buy a home pregnancy test kit without being recognized. "Shadow," she said, "I'm probably agonizing over nothing. Stress could be the problem, right?"

The spaniel woofed and lapped at her cheek.

That did make her laugh and gave her momentary calm.

She arrived before eight. Other shoppers were already in the pharmacy. Jewell rolled her pickup windows down a couple inches to give Shadow air and slapped on a cowboy hat to hide her face as she went inside.

Cruising down an aisle advertising pregnancy test kits, she was astonished to see five or six kinds. Knowing nothing about any of them since she dealt with pregnant animals, not humans, she took a moment to read a few boxes. All worked similarly. Pee in a cup, moisten a stick, wait one to five minutes, and lines either appeared or didn't. A digital type showed a display with the words *pregnant* or *not pregnant* in a frame. That seemed less likely to be disputable, so she chose that one. Then, not wanting to look desperate to a clerk, she added toothpaste, hand lotion and dog treats to her basket.

Taking a deep breath, she passed through the checkout.

Back at her vehicle, Jewell fed Shadow a treat. The smell of the open packet of jerky caused a resurgence of nausea. "This is crazy, Shadow. I need to take this test before I go berserk. Rather than drive home, I'll stop and fill my gas tank at a station I know has clean restrooms. In a few minutes I can end these silly worries."

The dog pawed her arm, whining for another treat.

"You can have one after I pump gas and get a key to the ladies' room."

At the station she topped off her tank and managed to joke with the attendant who provided a key to the locked bathroom.

Leaving her hat in the cab, she settled Shadow with another treat and entered the restroom on mushy legs. She carefully followed the directions step-by-step. There wasn't room to pace while waiting out the time. But she hummed and twice washed her hands. Still, it struck a blow when the word *pregnant* appeared in the square.

A baby. She was going to have a baby.

Fighting dizziness, she stuffed everything back in the pharmacy bag and tossed the damning evidence in the trash can by the door. She returned the key to the office but sat dazedly in her pickup, unable to get under way because she was so rattled.

Shadow lay down and placed his head on her lap, keening as if he knew something wasn't right.

Jewell absently rubbed his silky ears. It wasn't that she didn't think she had what it took to be a mother. She did. Nor was it that she couldn't afford to support a child on her own. She could. But many in the area were pretty conservative. The lion's share of her work was out on the range among men. Quite a few were older. She'd had to earn respect and trust as a veterinarian. Some had been slow to accept her. She hated the thought of them talking about her behind her back. And men did gossip.

A man drove in, gassed up his truck and went inside. He came out carrying a pack of cigarettes and detoured by her pickup to tap on her window.

"You okay, little lady?" he asked after Jewell ran down the glass a ways.

"I'm fine." She offered a weak smile. "Just doing some heavy meditating."

He tipped his cowboy hat and strode off. She judged him to be a man about her dad's age. One of the chivalrous kind she had concerns about. And Lordy, how would she explain this to her parents? She was their only child, and they still doted on her.

Not ready to return home to where her answering machine might hold calls from some of those same ranchers she wasn't prepared to face, she went out to the forest to see the snowy owls.

Shadow fell asleep on the drive. Leaving him, she quietly climbed out and sat on a log she often utilized when counting chicks. Since breeding occurred in May and June, there wouldn't be new babies. Really, though, today she needed to sort out her own life.

She'd been seated only a few minutes when two owls swooped from the trees, one a black-and-white female, the other her snow-white mate. They circled her, probably to see if she was a predator. Their appearance was a good omen, and seeing them acting so protective of their nests moved her. Snowies were good parents, as she would also be.

This pregnancy was a gift. She couldn't have Saxon in her life, but by having his child, she'd have part of him. That thought simultaneously lifted her spirits and depressed her. Oh, but she'd have to tell him. Her spirits sank again. When or how presented a bigger problem. Not that telling him would change anything. She'd never tie him down. He had to be free to pursue his career. She needed to assure him his child would have the love and the stability of growing up in Snowy Owl Crossing.

Shadow woke up. Jewell heard him barking. The noise made the owls anxious. They dived at her windshield. Standing, she dusted off the seat of her jeans. Feeling slightly better than when she had first seen the results of the pregnancy test, she went to quiet her excited pet.

On her way home she stopped at a grocery store and bought ready-made salads. She headed to Leland's with one and phoned Doreen to tell her.

"I thought we agreed you'd make supper and I'd do lunch," Doreen said.

"I was at the store and thought I'd save you leaving the café today. I have a Cobb salad and I'm parking at his house right now."

"In that case, tell him I'll be there tomorrow at one." Lila's mom hung up and Jewell was left wondering if she'd stepped on Doreen's toes. Oddly, the woman seemed to have forgotten that tomorrow was her daughter's wedding.

Jewell didn't worry for long, as Leland greeted her quicker than last time.

"I appreciate this, girl. Yesterday Doreen brought me

tomato soup. I swear I don't know why I'm so peaked. I hardly do any work around the ranch."

"Maybe rest is what you need after raising and selling hay and milo for years. I'll nab you some of Doreen's hors d'oeuvres at Lila's wedding tomorrow and bring them by when it's over. You kick back and watch TV."

"And cake? Will you bring wedding cake? Lila invited me, but I'm saving my suit to be buried in."

"What a thing to say," Jewell chided. "Eat this and feel better, okay?" She gave him an awkward hug.

The old man waved her away without promising anything.

THE MORNING OF Lila and Seth's wedding, the bridesmaids and bride met at Mindy's hair salon. The minute Jewell stepped through the door, the smell of coffee hit her. She hadn't been able to tolerate drinking it for a couple weeks, and now she knew why. She needed to break her news to her friends. However, this was Lila's big day. Calmer for having learned the source of her head and stomach issues, Jewell could wait to share with everyone until Lila returned from her brief honeymoon.

Because she'd been too restless again to sleep, Jewell had pulled pictures of Saxon off his agent's website and had printed two flyers advertising his concert. The copies she brought along weren't the first she'd printed. Those ended up splotched with tears she hadn't been able to control.

She hugged everyone, then showed them the flyers.

"Do we have to pick one?" Tawana asked, peering at both over Lila's shoulder.

"Wow, he's hot looking," Mindy exclaimed, taking her turn viewing the pages.

"He is," Myra agreed. "I only vaguely remember him since I didn't go to school here. I just spent summers with my grandparents. I have to trust you all that he's as talented as he is good-looking."

"He's always been super talented," Jewell said defensively. "Now he has the polish of a major artist."

"Right," Lila muttered. "You'd know since you attended his concert back east. You said it was cut short by a storm. But you saw some of it? How was he received?"

"The theater was sold out in spite of an impending hurricane."

"That bodes well for us," Tawana said. "How soon can we get these flyers?"

"I have a stack in my pickup," Jewell admitted.

"Great. We'll hand them out at the wedding to everyone except Lila, who'll only have eyes for Seth." She nudged the bride-to-be and grinned.

Mindy whipped her salon chair around. "Since that's settled, who wants to be first for roses? No one has said anything about mine. I fixed my hair to show you."

"Too many things happening, but I noticed and love how it looks. Me first," Myra volunteered.

Working swiftly even amid all their chatter, Mindy finished by eleven.

"Perfect," Lila noted after checking her watch. "Let's head to my place. We should arrive about the same time as our dresses."

On the drive Jewell began to feel woozy. Myra had specifically mentioned suffering morning sickness.

However, Jewell's bouts came any time of day or evening. Now she worried that something might be wrong with her pregnancy.

The friends converged on Lila's B and B en masse. Afraid the coffee latte and half a biscotti she'd consumed at Mindy's were threatening to come up, Jewell detoured to the downstairs bathroom.

Myra, apparently, had the same idea. She laughed. "Liquid runs right through me these days. Gosh, Jewell, you're gagging. Are you sick?"

"Please let me go in first. Then I'll explain." She rushed through the door and barely made it in time to empty the meager contents in her stomach. Instantly relieved, she washed her face and hands, then went out. "Myra, I don't have anything you can catch. I have to swear you to secrecy, but I need your advice."

"Sure." Lowering her voice, Myra drew a cross over her heart. "Hold that thought. I'll be right out."

She returned before Jewell had time to reconsider. She plunged ahead with her story, admitting how she'd impulsively slept with Saxon. "He used protection," she murmured. "But the test was positive and I have symptoms. I need your advice on an OB." Biting her lip, Jewell watched Myra's eyes grow rounder. Wishing she'd waited to tell the whole group together, Jewell backed up a few steps and bumped into Lila's mom, who emerged from the shadows of an empty dining room.

"Sorry," Doreen said, sidestepping Jewell. "I was checking to see that the table is ready for the reception before bringing in the cake."

Jewell shifted toward Myra, then stopped Doreen. "I

told Leland I'd bring him some of your hors d'oeuvres. He asked for cake, too. Should I take him a slice? You said he needs to eat healthier."

"Let me take him food. I'll be packing everything up when we wind down. It'll be easier for me to swing past his house. Maybe you could take him lunch tomorrow. Sundays at the café are always hectic. Without Lila, I'm shorthanded, too."

"That's fine by me. Gosh, I almost forgot I volunteered to board Lila's dog. I'll be happy to skip seeing Leland today. So you haven't replaced Lila yet?"

"No. But Tawana recommended a friend from the reservation. I plan to interview her next week."

"That sounds hopeful. Well, Myra and I need to go dress."

Doreen hurried off then, but Myra grabbed Jewell's arm. "Did she hear us? I love her, but she tends to gossip."

"We were practically whispering."

"True. I know we need to go, but I'll give you the name of my OB. Shayla Archer's office is next door to Dr. Rice. She's great. Tell her I sent you."

"Thanks. Will she judge me?"

"Oh, Jewell. We've evolved past such old-fashioned thinking."

"I can't help but worry what clients will say when they find out."

"When do you plan to tell the other Artsy Ladies?"

Jewell took a deep breath. "After Lila gets back. Maybe when we all get together to finalize our jobs for the concert. You know, who sets up chairs. Ushers. Sells tickets."

"It's really going to happen. Oh, but…wow, you'll see Saxon. I'm so sorry, Jewell. None of us had any inkling you were…"

"I didn't know, Myra. It's okay. Difficult as it'll be, Saxon has to be told."

Myra looked unsure as she mounted the stairs.

"There you two are," Lila exclaimed. "We thought you'd gotten lost."

"Side trip to the ladies' room," Myra explained, and her explanation wasn't questioned.

As the clock ticked nearer two, Myra's mother and Seth's mom helped the last two bridesmaids into their gowns. Mindy did their makeup, all while the friends' happy chatter reached unbelievable decibels.

A sharp rap at the door had the group quieting. Rory stuck his head in the room. "Mom, the minister said it's time to start. Uncle Zeke said the moms up here need to go down and take their seats. But not you. Remember, you go with me when Aaron Younger plays that special song on his keyboard."

Seth's and Myra's mothers slipped out past the boy. Mrs. Odell leaned back to say the bridesmaid escorts were lined up and waiting on the landing.

Each friend hugged Lila, then Rory, as they stopped to pick up their bouquets.

"Mom? Why are you crying?" Rory rushed to her side.

"These are happy tears, honey. I'm so blessed to share this wonderful day with you, Memaw, and all my best friends." She picked up the lovely cascade of peach roses chosen by her husband-to-be.

"Yeah. And I'm getting a dad. I hear the music. Let's hurry so you can say 'I do' like you did at practice. Then we can eat."

Laughing, Lila smudged away tears and slid her arm through Rory's. "Gosh, you've grown taller."

Jewell waited at the door, then preceded them to the landing where they'd watch bridesmaids and groomsmen traverse the winding old staircase, affixed with shimmering satin bows.

Jewell and Eric Odell were first to descend. Looking down, she suffered a wave of dizziness and tightened her hold on Eric's arm.

"Are you okay?" he queried out of one side of his mouth. "Why you ladies wear killer high heels is beyond me."

That let Jewell smile and the bout passed. Being first down, she was able to fully experience the wedding pageantry. Yet she suffered a twinge of gloom, because the ritual would never be hers. It was great Lila had found love for a second time, but Jewell knew in her heart now that while she'd be mother to Saxon's child, they'd be tied together forever, but never through marriage.

Aaron played a standard version of Pachelbel's Canon in D as a glowing, beaming mother and son made their walk into Seth's waiting arms.

For Jewell, the rest of the wedding and reception drifted by in a blur. She mingled for a discreet time, then changed out of her finery into jeans. Snagging Rory, she let him know she was taking his dog home with her.

"Aren't you staying to see Mom and Dad open presents?"

She shook her head. "Tell your mom I have animals in my infirmary. I'll see her when she gets back from Billings."

"I'd help with Ghost, but I probably shouldn't get white hair all over my new suit."

"I'll be fine on my own, Rory. I saw him out in the backyard. I'll take him through the side gate and you can let guests know it's okay if they want to gravitate out onto the back porch."

"What's *gravitate*?"

"It means they can move this crowded reception out of the cramped dining room," Jewell said, ruffling his red hair.

GHOST AND SHADOW hit it off even better than Jewell hoped. She had a call on her clinic answering machine from a rancher who either wasn't invited to the wedding or chose not to go. He had a mare in labor for what he considered too long. Grabbing her kit, Jewell left the dogs playing in her fenced backyard. Frankly, it felt good to return to a routine.

The mare delivered a handsome colt with only a little help from Jewell and the owner.

Driving home, she rolled down her pickup window and breathed in the cool, fresh air. It probably wouldn't be fun working through a Montana winter while pregnant. But pioneer women had gone before her. If she went full-term, she figured her baby would arrive around Saint Patrick's Day. On Monday she'd make an appointment with Myra's OB. That should calm her concerns.

That night she shared her bed with two dogs.

Shortly before dawn she crawled out and let the bed hogs have the whole mattress.

Her Sundays were generally light. Jewell spent the morning preparing a homemade soup in her Crock-Pot. It'd be perfect to share with Leland since she told Doreen she'd take him lunch. Feeling domestic, she got out her bread maker and soon the smell of baking bread had the dogs awake, clamoring for breakfast.

She fed them and turned them out to play in the backyard.

By noon the soup was done enough to separate into covered bowls. She sliced and wrapped half the loaf of herb bread and loaded it and the soup into her pickup.

Partway down Leland's lane she passed Eddie Four Bear tilling a fallow field. She waved, but he didn't respond. Glancing in her rearview mirror, she saw he wore big earphones that tuned him out to the noise of his tractor and obviously her pickup, too.

It was quiet around Leland's house. He often parked his old pickup in the barn, so its absence didn't mean he wasn't home. He could've gone to church. She hadn't dropped by on a Sunday before.

Crawling out to make sure he was home, she left the food. She climbed the porch steps and opened the screen to knock. It was such a nice morning she was surprised he didn't have his door open to let in fresh air.

The door swung open and he stepped out on the

porch. He was dressed except for slippers. But he looked pasty white and drawn.

"Jewell. I wasn't expecting anyone. Excuse the slippers."

"No problem. I brought you homemade soup and bread for lunch." She gestured toward her pickup. "Let me fetch it."

"Do come in. I want to talk to you about something that's come to my attention."

He turned his back to go inside, then toppled over, landing with a sickening thud at her feet.

"Leland!" Jewell sank to her knees and rolled him onto his back. She pressed two fingers to his neck and thought she felt a tiny pulse. She set one ear against his chest. It didn't rise or fall. After a second check of his wrist she barely felt a pulse and knew time was precarious. Lamenting having left her phone in her pickup, she prepared to start CPR.

Their town had a volunteer fire department. A few of the men had gone through EMT training. However, she had no way to reach them. She ripped open Leland's shirt, settled the heels of her hands midway down his breastbone and began compressions.

He wasn't a large man, but he was barrel-chested. It took all her strength to depress his chest. Sweat trickled between her breasts.

Unable to stop tears that blinded her, she threw her weight into rapid, stiff-armed pumps.

She sensed time slipping away. Exhaustion sapped her strength. Yet even as her arms grew numb, she imagined she heard the growl of a motor close by.

She couldn't turn to look. She had to trust it wasn't a figment of her imagination. Blessedly, she heard heavy footsteps pounding up the porch steps moments before her arms gave out. "Thank heavens. Is that you, Eddie? Please help me."

What almost shocked her into stopping was the deep male voice that demanded, "Jewell, what in hell happened? Here, let me take over."

Saxon. It couldn't be!

She must be hallucinating. Probably so, since her head was spinning. However, the man in the flesh landed next to her on his knees and placed his larger hands on top of hers. "I trust you've phoned for help."

"I left my phone in my pickup," she mumbled. "I'll get it."

"Leave this to me. Call quickly. There's still a fire department, right?"

"Yes." She vaulted to her feet and ran to get her phone. After punching in the fire department number, she reached the captain. "Dan, Jewell Hyatt. I'm at Leland Conrad's. He's collapsed. Hurry—he's either had a stroke or a heart attack."

Sinking down next to Saxon, she muttered, "Dan says they'll be here in five minutes. Wh-what… How did you get here?"

"Airplane and car. So it's true he has a bad heart? That's what Fred's sources thought. Why didn't you tell me?" he asked, all the while continuing compressions as fast as Jewell had but harder.

"I didn't know his problem until Doreen Mercer said

she saw him last week at the clinic making an appointment to see a new heart doctor in town."

At a distance, sirens wailed. As the sound grew louder, Jewell stood and waved frantically. She saw Eddie yank off his earphones, stop his tractor and sprint toward them. "What's wrong?" he asked, panting as he leaped up on the porch. "Can I help?"

"Maybe." Jewell knelt again. "Look, did his eyelids flutter?"

"I didn't see anything." Saxon didn't relax his ministrations until three men in firefighter gear, one depositing a square black kit on the porch and another a stretcher, scooted him aside.

"We got this, buddy. Ralph, start an IV. Shall I hit him with the paddles?"

"Jewell, who's his doctor?" the fire captain asked as his colleague swabbed Leland's vein and expertly stuck in a needle. The third man kept compressing Leland's chest.

"The new heart specialist in town," she murmured.

"Hamlin," said the man who'd started the IV.

Leland moaned and tried to lift his arm.

"He's coming around. Let's move him to the aid car for transport," said the fireman who'd opened the defibrillator case. "If need be, we'll use the paddles en route to the hospital," he added, closing it again. "You three can follow to give particulars. Jewell, notify Doc Hamlin about this episode."

The captain leaned down. "Hey, Leland, it's Dan, Ralph and Porter. We're taking you to the hospital. Jewell's going to call your doc."

"Ralph, take good care of him," Jewell implored as she followed them to the steps, then stopped.

Leland blinked, but his eyes looked glassy and unfocused. In a barely audible voice he said, "Call Jim Weiss."

She inclined her head and the burly team carried Leland off at a lope. She gripped her phone, found a number for Dr. Hamlin and left an urgent message with his answering service.

"Who's Jim Weiss?" Saxon inquired when she clicked off.

She shrugged.

Eddie Four Bear scraped back his straight black hair. "I've gotta go back to ready the field before rains move in. If you don't know Weiss, Jewell, he's the lawyer Leland called to set up the contract giving Aaron and me permission to share crop till spring." Eddie jumped to the ground without touching the steps, leaving Jewell and Saxon gawking after him.

Chapter Seven

"Ride with me to the hospital," Saxon entreated Jewell.

Still shaking, she said, "You go on ahead. I have soup and bread in my pickup to put in Leland's fridge. I'll lock up, then try to locate a number for Mr. Weiss."

"Where's the hospital? I don't recall there being one in Snowy Owl Crossing," Saxon admitted.

"It's still the one for the tri-cities. Go to the highway and turn right. Once you reach the city limits, you'll see blue signs directing you to the hospital."

"I'll wait and follow you. Let me get the food while you track down his lawyer. Why do you suppose he wants him?"

Jewell sighed. "I've no idea." It was plain Saxon wasn't budging. "I'll get the food, then worry about finding his lawyer." She hurried to her pickup, then retrieved the soup and bread and didn't look at him as she swept past him into the house. He wasn't paying attention anyway. He leaned on the porch railing, tapping the face of his cell phone.

When she came out again, brandishing a key to lock the door, Saxon stuck his phone in her face. "Here's

Weiss's office number. Seeing how it's Sunday, I doubt he's there. Maybe it will connect to an answering service."

Tucking Leland's house key in her pocket, Jewell dug out her phone. Looking at Saxon's display, she entered the number on her keypad. "It is a service," she mouthed upon reaching a recording. "This is Jewell Hyatt, Mr. Weiss. I'm Leland Conrad's neighbor. He collapsed at his ranch and has been taken to the tri-cities hospital. He requested someone contact you. I'm not sure if he wants you to go there, but your name was the first thing he said after coming around." She hung up, sighed a bigger sigh and started down the steps.

"Hey, why the cold shoulder?" Saxon hollered. "You ran out on me in Maryland, not the other way around. And I left you a message at your clinic number, but you never bothered calling me back."

The weight of Leland's incident coupled with Saxon's surprise arrival, plus knowing what she had to tell him, was almost too great a burden. "I'm worried," she called out over her shoulder. "You should be, too. Can we stop wasting time?" She climbed into her pickup and started it without waiting to see if Saxon left the porch.

He did, and his big SUV with rental plates stayed on her bumper from the ranch road all the way to the hospital.

On the relatively short drive she had barely managed to get her own heart rate down. Since Saxon had shown up several weeks early for his concert, she consoled herself that she had ample time to discuss their personal situation. Maybe she'd even wait until after his show. What if he got mad and took off, leaving them in the lurch after they'd advertised and sold a lot of tickets? She thought Mindy had already presold a ticket to every woman who had a standing appointment at her beauty shop.

She shouldn't be worrying about the performance considering Leland's iffy condition. Jewell doubted he'd been cognizant enough to recognize Saxon. His eyes had opened only once and briefly. She hoped seeing Saxon at the hospital wouldn't set him back. Their relationship had always been like water and oil. There was no explanation for why suddenly today Saxon showed up at his uncle's ranch. How could she wish he hadn't when he'd probably saved Leland's life.

On reaching the hospital, Jewell parked and saw Saxon pull in beside her. He tossed a gray cowboy hat aside and climbed out. He was dressed more like a regular cowboy and not glitzy like he'd been onstage.

They entered the hospital side by side without speaking. But then Saxon hung back and let her inquire about Leland's whereabouts at the reception desk.

"Are you family?" the clerk asked. "Mr. Conrad was admitted to ICU. Dr. Hamlin's there. He left word to send the patient's family up."

"We are family," Saxon inserted before Jewell could say she was only a neighbor.

"Fourth floor. Check in at the desk when you get off the elevator."

They caught the elevator along with several other people. All the others got off on lower floors. Saxon remained silent. The only thing Jewell said was, "We should silence our phones."

Both took care of that detail as they stepped out of the elevator. Saxon walked over to the desk. "We're here to see Leland Conrad," he told a nurse seated behind a computer. "His doctor left word downstairs that we were to come up straightaway. I'm Saxon Conrad. This is Jewell."

"The nursing team has left his room. Dr. Hamlin's still with him," she noted. "You'll find them in pod 403. Signal the doctor. He'll decide if it's okay for you to go into the room." She pointed across a narrow corridor where Jewell saw several glassed-in cubicles all opening out to this nursing station.

"Thank you," Jewell mumbled, feeling her jitters return as she crossed the tile floor. She wished Saxon would go on ahead, but he didn't. The doctor glanced up as her shadow fell across the room and gestured for them to come in. Jewell went to stand at the end of the bed.

Stopping short, Saxon braced one shoulder against the wall.

Leland looked small in the high railed bed, but Jewell was relieved to see his color was better. Probably because he had oxygen being fed into his nose. And two IV drips in his left arm. She actually found comfort in the steady beep of his heart monitor.

"I'm Jewell Hyatt," she told the doctor in a whisper. "Leland's next-door neighbor. The receptionist said family could come up, but I was first on the scene at his ranch when he had his attack."

"Ah, the woman who saved my patient's life." The doctor smiled.

"That was Leland's nephew, Saxon," she said, jerking a thumb toward him. "It was a miracle he showed up when he did and took over CPR. Is Leland conscious?" If so, he hadn't yet opened his eyes or given any indication he knew they were there.

Just then he stirred and squinted around. "It is you," he said, gazing past Jewell. "I woke in a fog and saw firemen trussing me up. But I glimpsed you and thought you were Bernadette. So I figured I'd died." The old man closed his eyes again.

Saxon straightened away from the wall but frowned and hooked his thumbs over a silver buckle on his wide leather belt. "You thought I was my mother?"

"As a kid, you were her spitting image," the man in the bed croaked. His eyes cracked open a slit. "Now I see a blend of her and my brother. I'm glad you're here before I kick the bucket. I have things to atone for. Did someone get hold of Jim Weiss?"

The doctor shook his head vigorously. "You aren't kicking any bucket, Leland. I'm scheduling you for surgery later today. After I repair your mitral valve, you can live another twenty years or more."

"I'm not having any damned pig or bovine heart," sputtered his patient.

Dr. Hamlin rolled his eyes. "It's a valve, you stubborn old goat. For as long as you've put off this surgery, you deserve a gorilla valve. But as far as I know, they don't use those yet."

Leland did his best not to smile, but one sneaked out.

Partly shocked, Jewell swiveled her head between Leland and his combative young doctor. She was used to staid old docs who'd never challenged a patient that way. But maybe tough love was what Leland needed. She occasionally used it herself.

"Go on, Doc," the old man grumbled. "Beat it. Schedule the frigging procedure. I need to talk to my nephew and Jewell. Let Jim in, though. Someone phoned him, right?" he asked haltingly.

Jewell responded when Saxon didn't. "I left a message with his answering service. Perhaps Saxon and I should go, too, and let you rest before surgery. I don't mean leave altogether. We'll wait until you're out of recovery. Won't we, Saxon?" she said, pinning him with concern.

Slow to nod, nevertheless, Saxon did jerk his chin down.

The doctor studied one then the other. "Leland apparently has things he needs to get off his chest. I'm for anything that'll ease his mind prior to my operating on him." Turning to his patient, he said firmly, "I'll give you ten minutes. Talk fast, because ICU nurses are the best at following doctors' orders."

"Where's Weiss?" Leland fretted. "I need to change my will before I die, Doc."

Hamlin leaned over the bed. "I'm going to see that doesn't happen. You can contact your lawyer after you recover." He squeezed Leland's shoulder, strode out between Jewell and Saxon and angled toward the nursing station.

"Maybe I should go and let you two talk," Jewell said.

"No!" Saxon and his uncle spoke in unison.

Leland's gaze roamed over his nephew. "The closer I come to perdition, Saxon, the more remorse I suffer for the rotten way I treated you." He feebly lifted a hand and let it fall. "I'm ashamed." Tears slicked his pale eyes.

"Whatever the reason, let it go." Saxon cleared his throat. "I like to think I've matured enough to recognize I had a bad attitude back then, too. It's sufficient to know you recognize you should have done better as the adult in charge."

"Hush, and let me get this out," the old man rasped. "When you came to live with me, looking at me with your mother's eyes, I felt I was being punished a second time when I wasn't the one who'd done anything wrong." He tried to wave again, this time with the hand that held the IVs in his arm. Grimacing, he let it fall to his side.

Jewell rounded the bed and took his papery hand in hers. "Are you sure this can't wait? You stopped breathing earlier. Stress can't be helpful, Leland."

"This has festered in me far too long. The doc knows that."

Rocking back on his heels, Saxon crossed his arms. "What is it you imagine I did wrong? I was just a kid. I mean, if you're not taking blame, that only leaves me."

Leland huffed out a ragged breath. "You obviously aren't aware I was once engaged to marry Bernadette."

Saxon's eyes bugged. "My mother? You were engaged to my mother?"

"Yes." Leland licked his lips. "We, uh, put off our

wedding because of word my younger brother Myron was coming home from Vietnam."

Saxon moved closer to the side of the bed. "A case-worker who picked me up at school the day my folks died in that wreck later gave me a box of his medals. He never talked about the war. I hadn't known he'd served in the Army. But…" Saxon's eyes darkened and Jewell saw how troubled they'd become. "But…you…" He tried to get something out and failed.

"Uh-huh. Now you're tripping close to the truth, which is…my brother came home an unrecognized hero like all Vietnam vets. He had wounds. As a nurse, Bernadette took care of him. Her note to me when they ran off to Vegas to get married claimed they'd fallen in love. They killed any belief I'd previously had about love." His voice dropped an octave and Jewell tightened her hold on his hand.

Saxon crossed his arms and stood stiffly.

"Myron attempted to call me several times after they moved to California. I always hung up on him."

"Like you did two weeks or so ago when I phoned you?" Saxon's lips thinned.

"Telephones, bah! If I'd told you this, you would've hung up on me. So listen up. I thought they had some nerve sending me your birth announcement. I ripped it to shreds. I was a bitter man. You think guilt didn't hit me like a ton of bricks when they were killed? It did. Yet when the court called on me as your only relative, all I could see was that I'd been double-slapped by fate." He tried to take a deep breath, and his voice faded. "You were the kid Bernadette should've had with me. That's a hard belief to live with."

Saxon whirled around and set both hands against the wall opposite Leland's bed, presenting his back to his uncle. Jewell, though, could see his jaw working convulsively, but he didn't say anything.

She wondered if she ought to go console him. But Leland still clung tightly to her hand. She felt anguish for both of them. She always had even without knowing the underlying cause.

"Jewell, the doc claims he'll fix my heart. What if he doesn't? Can you convince Hamlin that I need to change something in my will before I go under his knife?"

"Oh, Leland, you need to have faith. Look, I see the nurse coming. Our time is up. Be positive. We'll see you after you come out of recovery."

Saxon slowly turned around. "If you're worried that I expect you to leave me anything in your will, rest easy, because I don't."

"Saxon!" Jewell glared at him before eyeing the approaching nurse again.

"Well, right now you're the sole beneficiary." Leland seemed to struggle to breathe in enough oxygen to say more.

Patting his hand, Jewell slipped hers out and smiled at the nurse, who'd reached the open door. "We've got to leave. Leland, Saxon came to give a concert on Labor Day. You men will have plenty of time to discuss your will, or whatever else, when you're better."

"No." The old man's voice strengthened. "Last month I added a codicil letting Eddie Four Bear and Aaron

Younger plant and harvest my fields this year. I've seen for a while, Saxon, that you're doing well. So now I want the ranch in total to go to your and Jewell's child. I need that spelled out."

The nurse motioned to Saxon and Jewell. "I'm sorry to cut this gathering short, but Dr. Hamlin wants his patient to rest until surgery."

Saxon leveled a scowl at her, then his uncle and finally Jewell. "It's plain something's affecting his mind. Maybe medication, or perhaps he needs more oxygen. You're right, old man, about me doing well. But since you're talking crazy, I wonder if anything you said about you and my parents is even true."

The minute she heard Leland's revelation, Jewell wanted to disappear. Sick dizziness coursed through her, but a vise held her tongue.

"Everything I said, Saxon, is assuredly true." Leland rolled his head on the pillow to stare at Jewell. "Am I wrong?" he probed. "Doreen brought food by my house after Lila's wedding. She swore she overheard you telling Myra Maxwell that you were going to have Saxon's baby. She said you asked Myra's advice about a doctor."

The furrows lodged between Saxon's brows deepened. He swung toward Jewell, his eyes bright with anger. "Before we go, Jewell, tell him that's impossible," he said as he brushed past the nurse. "We...ah... Well, suffice to say it's total bull."

Cringing, Jewell was slow to lift her quivering chin. "That's what I told myself for quite a while," she said softly. "When my symptoms didn't abate, I did a home pregnancy test. Don't ask me how, Saxon, but it's true."

She held up a hand. "You've no reason to be concerned or upset, though. I'll handle it by myself. And, Leland," she said, breaking eye contact with Saxon, "don't fret. I have a nice home for me and the baby and I do well with my practice, too. I'll be fine. Uh, we'll be fine," she murmured, curving a hand over her still-flat belly.

Turning, Saxon's voice rose. "Were you not going to tell me? Wait…what kind of a doctor were you asking about? I'll fight you to hell and back if you plan to get rid of my baby."

Jewell flew around the bed. "That's insulting. And lower your voice. For pity's sake, we're in ICU, and your uncle's in ill health." She shoved him out the door and addressed the nurse. "We've overstayed the time Dr. Hamlin authorized. Leland, relax. I'll…uh, we'll see you after surgery." Squaring her shoulders, she stormed past Saxon.

The nurse called to the retreating pair. "Dr. Hamlin has scheduled Mr. Conrad's surgery for five o'clock. You're welcome to wait in the family room on the fifth-floor surgery wing."

Saxon whirled and stuck his head back in the room. "I echo what Jewell said, except I'll support any kid of mine. I'll see you after you're out of recovery," he added, withdrawing again.

"Don't leave yet. I'm not finished. I, ah, have more to say." Leland's voice was a deep rumble. "It's the real reason I wanted to talk to you. Saxon. Saxon!"

His uncle's words battered Saxon's back, but he stepped up his pace and caught up to Jewell at the elevator.

"Go away," she hissed, stabbing the down button urgently.

He cast a glance around. "I know you missed lunch. At least, I assume so since you took soup and bread to Uncle Leland's house. I didn't stop along the way from the airport, either. Let's find the cafeteria and talk while we eat."

"Why would I want to talk to you?" She poked him in the chest. "Almost since I could walk and talk, I've gone above and beyond to save all injured or stray animals. How dare you suggest I'd callously abort a baby? My baby."

"And mine," he added calmly as the elevator doors slid open. Taking hold of her elbow, he made room for the two of them in a fairly full car. "The way you ran out on me in Maryland, how can I be sure you haven't changed from the girl…uh, woman I once knew and loved?" he admonished near her ear.

She glared and tried to jerk away because his comment garnered interest from other people in the car. But when he deliberately kept her from exiting at the lobby, she sighed and stopped tugging to extract her arm from his hand. According to a sign in the elevator, the cafeteria was in the basement. As upset as her stomach was, she very likely needed something to settle the churning.

When this time the doors opened to the clatter of dishes and the warm smell of food, Jewell did wrest out of Saxon's loosened hold. "If you don't mind," she said wearily, "I'd rather eat alone. I have enough trouble these days keeping nausea at bay."

He nudged her close to the wall to let another group

pass. "I'm sorry, Jewell. You've had time to absorb information that has blown up at me out of left field."

"But how dare you question my integrity in front of that nurse and Leland."

"I admit I jumped to the worst possible conclusion. Grab us a table. Tell me what you want to eat. I'll get it. So much has hit me I need to sit awhile and unpack it all."

"I understand that. I really do. My nerves have been frayed since I blithely knocked on Leland's door and he stepped out on his porch and fell to the ground unconscious. I only felt a flicker of pulse in Leland's neck, Saxon. Even after I started CPR, I was scared to death he'd slipped away. If you hadn't shown up when you did, I doubt I would've saved him." Her lips trembled and tears filled her eyes.

Saxon hugged her awkwardly. "That's why you need time to sit and unwind, too. Please."

She blotted her eyes with a sleeve but eventually nodded and didn't object when he moved them along the hall. "I'll take a glass of milk." Stopping at the open double doors, she studied the busy room. "I see one table open in the corner. Is that okay?"

"Fine. But you need more than milk. It says on the board they have chicken noodle soup. Would you try a little if I get you a bowl?"

"Okay. And crackers. I remember Myra ate crackers the day we all met at the café. And she's pregnant with twins."

"Twins?" Saxon blinked and looked a tad shell-shocked. "I only caught part of that. You aren't saying you…uh… Are we having two…?"

"No, it's Myra who's having twins. Since I haven't seen a doctor, I've no way of knowing. And it's probably too soon to know that anyway. But it's not *we* anything, Saxon. Did you not hear me say you don't have to worry? I'll handle this alone."

A large man headed to the food line bumped them. Saxon pointed to the table. "Nab that quick. We will discuss this, Jewell," he promised through tight lips. Removing his hand from her back, he got in line behind the man who'd disrupted them.

Going to the empty table, Jewell set her elbows on the tabletop and buried her face in her hands. Dialing the hours back to the instant Leland fell over in front of her, she dredged up everything that had happened and attempted to calm nerves that left her a wreck. She could remind herself that everything had turned out okay—with the exception of Leland announcing her pregnancy to Saxon. There really wasn't any reason to pin her irritation about that on him. The culprit was Doreen Mercer. Myra had suggested Lila's mother might have overheard their private conversation. She should have heeded that and asked Doreen to keep silent until she had a chance to tell Saxon and the other Artsy Ladies.

Releasing a big sigh, she scrubbed her face a few times.

"Are you okay?" Saxon asked anxiously, setting a tray of food down in front of her. "I heard you sigh from two tables away. Do you need to find a place to lie down? You're ghost white. Jewell, don't fall apart now. We did everything humanly possible for Leland. He's alert and under the doctor's care."

Saxon set her soup, crackers and milk off the tray and did the same with his sandwich, his coffee and their utensils. "Try the soup while I stow this tray. You probably need a minute to destress and get something in your stomach." Standing, he held the tray but continued to study her worriedly.

"I'll be fine," she said, picking up the soupspoon. "There's no need to hover."

Heeding her, Saxon left and set the tray on a stack of empties. Returning, he sat across from her.

"I didn't mean to scold," she said. "This soup hits the spot. In looking back, I know it's lucky for Leland that I arrived when I did. And luckier still that you came when you did. He'd have died if he'd had his attack in his home with no one around. Then he never would've been able to tell you the story about him and your parents. It's obviously weighed heavy on his mind." She circled her spoon in the air. "By the way, I heard him call out that he had more to tell you. Why didn't you stay to hear what else he had to say?"

"The nurse said our time was up. Anyway, I wanted to catch you." Saxon bit into his sandwich. After swallowing, he said, "Do you think he was telling the truth? I mean, the blood supply to his brain could have been restricted. Or maybe he had a dream he thought was real."

"Last summer he asked if I knew how he could get in touch with you. He said it was important. I can't recall exactly when… Maybe around the time he listed his ranch to sell." Jewell opened a packet of crackers and ate one. "That might even have been when he started seeing a doctor in the next town. Doreen said as much the other day."

A nurse they both recognized as the one at the computer in ICU entered the cafeteria and looked around.

Jewell and Saxon both stiffened as she spotted them and sped toward their table. Trading a grim expression with Jewell, Saxon rose to meet her.

"Dr. Hamlin asked me to see if I could find you two," the woman said breathlessly. "Oh, wait…nothing's happened to your uncle. Sorry if my showing up like this has worried you. But he is refusing to sign the release to have the surgery."

"If this has to do with his insurance," Saxon said, "I only just got into town, and I really don't know anything about his private affairs."

The nurse shook her head. "Mr. Conrad provided all of that. This is another issue. If you'd rather discuss this in private, we can go back up to ICU."

Saxon tugged at his lower lip. "Feel free to speak in front of Jewell. I've not seen my uncle for years. She's his nearest neighbor and knows him as well as anyone."

"He's pretty tight-lipped," Jewell murmured. "What's the nature of his concerns?"

"Dr. Hamlin said Mr. Conrad is flatly refusing to consider going into a rehabilitation facility once he's released from the hospital."

"Is that necessary? Can he not just go home?" Saxon asked.

"He'll need dressings changed and his medications

monitored. Even assistance to and from the bathroom. And he won't be cleared to drive for some time. For this type of surgery, unless there's a caregiver in the home, patients are always sent to a rehab facility for a few weeks. He's stubbornly refusing to consider it."

Studying Jewell, the nurse said, "Dr. Hamlin noticed the EMT who brought Mr. Conrad in listed you and Dr. Hyatt as contacts. He wondered if you might be in a position to handle meal preparation and the other services I mentioned."

Jewell shook her head. "I'm sorry, but I'm a veterinarian. I have a busy practice. I may know a ranch wife or two who could possibly stay with Leland during the day. Offhand, I can't come up with anyone who'd be available for night duty."

"If he'll let me," Saxon said quietly, "I'll watch out for him. Lest you wonder why I qualified that by saying 'if he'll let me,' I'll be honest. Our relationship for many years has been rocky, to put it mildly."

Jewell burst out, "Don't you have stuff to do between now and Labor Day, when you're performing for an entire evening? And aren't you flying back to Nashville the following day?"

"So you are the country-western singer?" The nurse seemed excited. "One of the other nurses thought so. But she said you look different without a guitar and sparkly shirt. Are you really giving a show around here?"

Saxon dragged his glare back from Jewell. "I'm giving a benefit in Snowy Owl Crossing. I'm sure when we're done here, Jewell can tell you how to get tickets. Going back to my uncle…if he doesn't object to having me hanging around his ranch until he's back on his feet, I'm willing to help out."

Jewell stood up. "If you'll excuse me, while you and Saxon go upstairs to settle this with Leland, I'll go out to my pickup and get tickets for the concert. Perhaps it's crass to do this in the middle of Leland's crisis, but the money goes for a good cause. To secure a refuge for snowy owls."

"That'd be fantastic. Oh, but don't let me run you off from your meal. Mr. Conrad, if you'll come with me. I know Dr. Hamlin needs this resolved or he'll have to put off your uncle's surgery."

"While I'm outside, shall I make a few calls to see if I can find a caregiver before you ask Leland about Saxon sticking around? Lucky as we are to have him give our benefit, none on our committee would dream of tying up such a superstar."

The nurse raised hesitant eyes to Saxon, who'd followed her a few steps away from the table.

"Just get the tickets, Jewell," he grated. "I'll stay as long as it takes to get my uncle back on his feet."

Leaving Jewell openmouthed, Saxon hustled the nurse out of the cafeteria.

Chapter Eight

Jewell took her eyes off her phone as she reentered the hospital. Saxon stood by the elevator scanning the lobby. Her insides jolted every time he crossed her sight. She said goodbye to Sarah Watson and stuck her phone in her back pocket. It was her fourth call netting a no-dice answer on finding Leland a caregiver. Even though Saxon said he'd stay to help Leland, she didn't believe it. Not the way he was tied to his label. If they booked him to appear in Timbuktu, she couldn't imagine him telling them no.

"From the look on your face," Saxon said by way of greeting, "I'd say that phone call upset you."

"I struck out finding anyone to take care of Leland. I should've known. It's harvest season. Men work long hours putting up hay for the winter. Their wives are canning, freezing food, making jam, and otherwise helping around the ranch. Bigger cities have what are called *angel-service* home health workers. We'd have to ask if Leland's insurance would pay to bring someone in or if he could afford to pay privately."

"I wasn't kidding about looking after him. Is it that you don't feel I'll do a good job, or what? Ever since you brought me his letter, I've battled my conscience over hanging on to a grudge. Now that I'm here and see how ill he is, if nothing else, he deserves credit for having provided me a bed, food and schooling. If not for him, I'd have gone into foster care."

She watched him turn and punch the elevator button. "Saxon, what will it do to your career to drop it for however many weeks the doctor thinks Leland needs a caregiver?"

"My band's on break. I'd arranged to take some time off to write new songs. I can do it here as easily as in Nashville."

Her heart soared momentarily at the notion of seeing him around town for several weeks. As quickly it sank again. How easy would it be to get used to running into him? To start dreaming about him staying longer? Longer, like forever?

"You're awfully quiet," he said as they entered an empty elevator. "Are you worried I'm going to insist we talk about us and the baby? If so, good. Because when Leland's out of the woods, that will top my agenda."

Jewell stepped to the rear of the car, putting space between them. "I don't know what else there is to discuss," she said, bracing against the wall when the car lurched and started its ascent.

"Plenty," he ground out. "I'm still trying to process how in hell something went wrong back in Maryland. I'm not so naive that I don't know stuff can happen. That doesn't make accepting that it happened to me any easier. It's called protection for a reason. Is that home pregnancy test you said you took a hundred percent reliable?"

"Supposed to be." Her heart froze. He wasn't in any way happy about her news. "Where are we going?" she asked abruptly when he punched floor four. "Didn't the nurse say the surgical waiting room was on five?"

"When I went back with Nurse Kenyon, they were drawing blood on Leland. She told the charge nurse I agreed to help out. She said she relayed that, but he's insisting on seeing us again."

"Why would he need to see me? I could go on up to five."

"Maybe he feels bad about spilling the beans about… our accident. Frankly, he should. It's something that ought to be kept private between you and me."

Jewell wasn't sure how to take his statement, especially since her nerves were raw. "Listen! You needn't worry that news of *our accident*," she said testily, "will spread far enough to hurt your career. Snowy Owl Crossing isn't exactly a media metropolis. And you'll be long gone before I show, so neighbors or clients won't ask questions."

The door slid open and Saxon blocked Jewell's exit. "Stop it, okay? I'm not asking to be let off the hook. I can't fathom what kind of man you think I am. But I'm definitely not the ass you give every indication of believing now."

"Saxon," she entreated, "People want to get on the elevator."

"Oh, sorry." He stepped out and braced the door for

her exit. He continued to hold it open until the family waiting to get on did so.

"I'll find Nurse Kenyon and see if she still wants tickets," Jewell said. "You go on and see Leland. Also, I'm boarding animals at my clinic that need to be fed. I can go take care of them, then come back to wait for Leland to get out of recovery."

"Hang on until we know all is green-lighted for his surgery."

"I suppose. I have to say, Saxon, you're being way more magnanimous toward him than I expected."

Saxon scratched at the top of one ear and offered a minor shrug. "It's high time he and I moved on. I can't imagine how different my life might be had my parents not been killed, had I not moved to Snowy Owl Crossing and met you. I wouldn't have the career I have today."

Jewell exhaled fast. "Pardon me if I'm all mixed up when it comes to acknowledging any role I played in that, Saxon. I hate how our careers divided us."

"Like it or not, our pasts are pretty tied together."

She was tempted to say so were their present and their future, but they'd reached the ICU nursing station and Nurse Kenyon jumped up smiling, holding cash out for her five tickets. "A friend saw one of your flyers. She told me how much tickets are."

"Thanks for your support," Jewell murmured, stuffing the money in her pocket.

Turning to Saxon, the nurse said, "I assume you two want a word with your uncle. The charge nurse said he's asked a dozen times if she's seen you. He insists there's something more he needs to say ASAP."

Saxon grabbed Jewell's hand. "Don't leave. Come find out what's on his mind. Then you can go do your chores. Depending on whether it's tougher than hearing how my mom dumped him practically at the altar, I may need your moral support."

Jewell smiled at his genuine anxiousness. "All right. Maybe you should assure the charge nurse we won't do anything to upset him."

Saxon did just that.

"I'm relieved you've come again," she said. "He's cranky. And Dr. Hamlin's deciding what to do. We explained you'd agreed to help him out at home, but Leland is skeptical. Please reiterate that he won't be going to rehab."

"He could be stewing because he doesn't want my help. In any event, we'll make this a short visit. And I'll give you a verdict afterward."

"I know he's still asking to see his lawyer."

Rolling his eyes, Saxon set his hand on Jewell's waist and they crossed to Leland's cubicle. Before they reached it, she dug in her heels and gripped Saxon's arm. "Wait. This has nothing to do with Leland, but I can't forget this. Promise me you won't sing any songs at our concert like the one you sang in Maryland. Back there no one knew I was the jewel you found and lost. Here my friends will know. I can't handle them feeling sorry for me."

Saxon pursed his lips. "I wrote several songs for or to you. I happen to like them all. But I'll leave them out of my show. I can see it really bothers you."

"Honestly, I'm grateful that you agreed to give the benefit for the snowy owls."

His gaze slipped from her eyes to her mouth. "Uh… sure thing. Let's go on in. He sees us and is motioning to us," he said gruffly.

The minute they walked in, Jewell crossed and took Leland's hand. "We can't stay long. I'm running home to feed animals. I'll be back to see you after surgery."

"I'm not having it. I'm checking myself out. I'll take a cab home."

Jewell gasped. "Why would you entertain such foolishness? You almost died. Next time, if no one's around, you could. Saxon, tell him he can't do this."

"Bah!" Leland spat. "I know how they treat old geezers like me at a rehab place. Lost two friends at the one connected to this hospital. Only prolongs the inevitable. And the families are still paying huge hospital bills and rehab costs. Didn't do a lick of good, and both suffered mightily. I ain't goin'. Not that I don't have savings. I've even prepaid my funeral. Saw how smart it was that your dad did that in advance, Saxon. By the way, step closer so I don't have to shout. There's something else you need to know."

Saxon moved close to Jewell. "Save whatever it is. The charge nurse said she told you I volunteered to care for you at the ranch once you're discharged. Except for the owl benefit on Labor Day, I only need a few hours a day to compose new songs. I'm not the greatest cook, but I'm not the worst, either."

The old man's eyes watered. "You'd do that for me

after I neglected you and all but left you to raise yourself? They told me, but I thought they were lying."

Saxon shuffled uncomfortably. "I'm grateful you let me spend as much time at Jewell's house as you did. Her mom was a great cook. And you didn't skimp on basics. I never went hungry at school. You set up an account at the tractor supply store where I bought jeans and boots like the other kids wore. Then there's college. I'm guilty of pretending I'd continued in the agriculture program when I switched to music."

A muscle in Leland's weathered jaw jumped. "Enough! I'll take your word that you won't send me to rehab. Here's what else I need to say. Your folks had savings the court gave to me to raise you. I swear I never used one penny for myself."

Saxon waved off the concern. "I know you worked long hours in your fields."

"The way we butted heads, I figure you probably wonder why I started trying to contact you a year ago. I didn't want to say this in a letter that might have gone astray… Your parents both had life insurance, Saxon. You were their sole beneficiary. Each plan stipulated you couldn't access the money until age thirty. Peeved as I was over your leaving, I swear the policies skipped my mind. They're locked in the top drawer of my old rolltop desk. The key is in an empty juice can in my freezer. Your name's on the can. I didn't keep this from you to be mean. I forgot about them until I received a notice from the insurance company."

Jewell saw Leland had sagged against his pillows.

"It's only a year past his thirtieth birthday," she ventured. "Really, what harm's been done?"

"I'm rocked by the news," Saxon said. "But I'm here now. As young as my folks were, I doubt the policies amount to much."

"There's where you're wrong." Leland looked pained. "Each has a payout of five hundred thousand dollars. A million bucks doesn't buy what it used to, but it's nothing to sneeze at. I'm sorry. I should've flown to Nashville last year and run you to ground. Except that's when the doc said I had a bad ticker and couldn't fly. I needed you to come here."

Jewell choked at the amount. Saxon, too, reeled. But Leland rambled on with his apology until Dr. Hamlin charged into the room wearing a smile.

"So I just spoke to the charge nurse. She tells me the matter of rehab is settled. I assume that's what you're all discussing. However, if I'm going to get this guy to surgery at five, a prep team needs to come get started."

"I now believe my nephew will help out, if he's still of a mind to. I mean, you can take the money and get out of Dodge, son," Leland muttered, staring straight at Saxon.

He lifted his head. "I'm staying. And I'm not rummaging in your freezer or your desk on my own. I still need someplace to pen new lyrics. So are we cool now?"

This time Leland frowned. "We are if I make it."

"Dang. I'm going to ride out to Jewell's clinic with her. Don't you be cashing in your chips. I've still got a lot of holes when it comes to family. You're the only one who can fill in the blanks. Deal?"

"Deal," Leland said thickly. "Doc, I hope that spare part you ordered up for me comes from a tough old boar."

The young doctor grinned and winked at Jewell and Saxon, who spared small smiles as they left the room.

Riding with him to the lobby, Jewell wished she knew how to ask Saxon not to go with her. But he probably wanted a break, too. He'd been right earlier when he said he'd had a lot dumped in his lap, none of which he expected. Now he had even more.

The woman seated at the reception desk jumped up when they started to walk to the front doors. "Saxon. Saxon Conrad...could I get your autograph?" she asked, boldly coming around her desk with a pad and pen.

Saxon stopped and asked her name.

Jewell lost count of the women who kept appearing to crowd around him. He didn't seem the least bit bothered, but Jewell was antsy to leave.

"Is it like that everywhere you go?" she asked once he finally finished and they escaped to the parking lot.

"Mostly at performances. Sometimes when our buses pull into small towns if we stop to eat or get gas. Keeping fans happy is part of the job, Jewell. More than I imagined before I had records that climbed the charts."

"You didn't seem uncomfortable with all the attention," she remarked after unlocking her pickup.

He held her door until she climbed in. Then he circled the cab to hoist himself up into the passenger seat. "It's mostly fine. I don't like when someone gushes like a couple of those women did. That's embarrassing. More so on a tour, where often it's clear some would like more than my signature."

Jewell pondered his statement as she pulled out of the lot. "I'm a volunteer vet at the rodeo. I see the same thing happen to cowboys on the circuit. It's never been my impression that too many dislike the attention."

"It gets old. I can't speak for other performers, but label handlers push their rising stars to mingle. Then they freak out if something gets out of hand."

"Huh. Will they freak out over me?"

"No," he said quickly. "Don't worry."

"You said that like someone who doesn't believe it." She turned off the highway onto a gravel road. "Hey, look to your right. You'll see my clinic. I renovated my folks' garage and barn into an office and surgery facility. But a lot of my work is out on ranches."

"You painted the house. I like the cream siding and the dark brown trim. I know your parents moved to a warmer climate. I bet you miss them."

"Yes. They used to visit me at Christmas. But because I get calls to see sick cows and horses during harsh winters, the last two holidays my folks begged off. They also claim flights to Billings get diverted or canceled." She parked and gestured toward the infirmary. "After I see to the cat I'm monitoring, we'll feed the dogs in the house."

From the time they exited the vehicle, they could hear the dogs barking.

"Are they yours?" Saxon asked. "You used to always talk people into taking strays you found, or that found you."

"That howl is Lila's dog. He's a big yellow Lab. White, really. Hence his name of Ghost. The sharper bark is a spaniel I found cowering in my bushes when I returned from my trip east. I posted flyers. No one has claimed him. I tried not to get attached, but I couldn't help it. I named him Shadow, because he trails me everywhere." She shrugged.

Saxon wandered around looking at her setup while she fed the cat, checked its stitches and cuddled the animal for a bit.

"Daisy's ready to go home." She led the way to the house. Saxon stood aside while she unlocked her kitchen door. They were both nearly bowled over and licked to death by two excited dogs who'd come in through a still-flapping doggy door.

"Hey, they're giving you the most attention." Jewell pretended to pout at Saxon. "Here, you feed them while I phone Daisy's owner and arrange a time tomorrow for pick up." She opened a cupboard and handed him a bag of kibble, then made her call.

He poured the bowls full and drew fresh water at the sink without Jewell asking.

"You're kind of handy," she remarked after ending her conversation with Daisy's owner. "Oh, I see I have messages on my answering machine. If you'd like instant coffee or tea, the fixings and cups are in the cupboard by the microwave." She pointed with one hand and hit Playback on her machine with the other.

Tawana's voice boomed out. "Eddie came by from Conrad's ranch saying Leland collapsed. He said Saxon showed up and you two saved Leland. Since you aren't answering your cells and I'm not catching you at home, I hope you're not dealing with worse news. Call me when you can. By the way, the country station I listen to was full of rumors about Saxon sneaking off to meet an old girlfriend. His rabid fans were in a tizzy until his agent said he's off writing new songs. Is any of that true? Incidentally, we've sold six hundred tickets. I hate to ask what happens if Saxon's uncle, ah…doesn't make it? I hope you hear this and get back to me." Tawana hung up.

Jewell looked everywhere but at Saxon as the next caller began talking over the ding of the microwave. Doreen Mercer came on sounding frantic.

Saxon removed a steaming cup of coffee and eyed Jewell, who kept listening to Doreen's pleas. "…I'm tied up at the café until eight tonight. Porter stopped for coffee. He said Leland had a heart attack. I pray he's okay. I'm worried sick, but can't raise you on your cell. I phoned the hospital. Since I'm not related, no one will even verify he's there."

Jewell dug her phone out of her pocket. "I forgot I silenced it at the hospital," she mumbled. "Doreen sounds panicked. But I'm still steamed at her for gossiping to Leland about my…uh…condition. What's to say it wasn't her tattletales that caused his collapse?"

Saxon stepped around the counter and hovered over Jewell. "Stop rambling about Doreen. Don't you really want to ask me about Tawana's concern?"

"She's worried because she talked our group into contacting you."

"I'll do your benefit no matter what else comes up."

"Such as… What else might come up, Saxon? An old girlfriend?"

"It's you they're referring to. Your showing up in Maryland caused a stir among my band. I didn't explain us." He gestured with his mug. "I'll have to let Fred Harmon know I may need more time off to care for Leland. He's sure to give me grief. He's positive my uncle popped up to fleece me, which would cause a tabloid nightmare. In case you wonder why I phoned you after the way you ran out on me, that's why. You were the only person I knew of who might find out why, after so many years, he seemed desperate to see me." Pausing, he took a bigger swig of coffee.

"Saxon, I… Well, won't they feel like fools when you inform them Leland really wanted to make you a millionaire?"

"A million is chump change to Fred, and I sometimes earn that per tour. Actually, I've no intention of telling them about any of this. I have a right to my privacy."

Jewell's hackles ticked up. "So you're glad Snowy Owl Crossing is way off the map of country-western media."

"That is lucky. Hey, do you want coffee? It's not bad for instant."

Jewell shook her head. "Coffee upsets my stomach," she said offhandedly.

Shadow trotted up and butted his head against Saxon's leg. Bending, he rubbed the dog's ears. Ghost ran over, nosing in for his share. After Saxon gave attention to both animals, he dumped the rest of his coffee in the sink and rinsed the mug. "Unless you have more to do here, let's head back to the hospital. It's almost five. I'd like to be there when Leland goes into the operating room."

"Sure." After gathering her house key and cell phone, Jewell loved on the dogs, then told them to stay. Her mind was in a muddle over Saxon's careless reference to her. Not that she wanted him to tell the world about them. Neither did she appreciate being relegated as a hidden problem.

She'd barely driven away when he faced her and slid an arm over the back of her seat. "In a matter of hours you've heard my life dissected about every way possible, including personal stuff I didn't know. Isn't it time we talk about you?"

"Me?" She glanced at him, startled. "You saw my clinic, the house, and you met my dog. With all the hours you spent with my family, you should know that compared to yours, my life is boring."

"Jewell," he said gently, "it's time we talk about the baby."

"What about it? I said we won't interfere with your life, Saxon."

He ran a finger down the side of her face, forcing her to take her eyes off the empty country road to look at him. "If you know me like you should, you know that's not possible. It's nothing a guy likes to admit, but how often did you catch me crying over losing my parents? Yet you seem to believe I'd walk away from a kid I had a part in creating."

Tightening her hands on the steering wheel, Jewell returned her teary gaze to the road. "This is different. Your mom and dad were ripped away from you in a terrible accident. Our lives aren't like that. Your home is a bus, for pity's sake. I have roots here. Deep roots. Logically, which of us is better situated to raise a child?" She pulled up at the stop sign and flexed her fingers around the wheel before turning onto the highway that would take them back to the hospital.

"It's plain you've had time to give this serious thought. I know you said you intended to tell me while I was here. It's equally plain you never intended to give me any say in the matter."

"I take full responsibility for what happened the night of the storm, Saxon."

"Really?" Tossing back his head, he gave a snort. "You're claiming immaculate conception?"

"Don't be a smart-ass. Can't we be adult about this?"

"That depends if your idea of being adult and mine are the same."

She fidgeted, chewing on her lower lip. "Can we at least get through one crisis at a time? I can't talk about this while we wait to hear how Leland's surgery turns out. Then you'll be looking out for him as he recovers. I'm willing to set aside a day before you leave to discuss how our divided obligations affect our baby."

"That's darned decent of you," Saxon drawled, giving an irritated eye roll as she drove into the hospital parking lot and stopped next to his rental vehicle.

"I don't know what you expect of me," Jewell said, shoving the gear shift into Park.

"Seems I recall telling you at least twice what I hoped could be our joint future."

"Oh, right. Around here they still call what you last

offered *shacking up*. I can't see anything's changed, Saxon. My clinic isn't portable."

He let her shut off the engine before adding softly, but with steel, "I'd say you being pregnant with my baby changes a whole lot."

She pocketed the pickup key, rubbed her neck and sighed. "We have the results of a seven-dollar digital test I took in the bathroom at a gas station. I haven't even seen an OB. Can we at least shelve talk until after I see a doctor and get professional advice as to what to expect next?"

"Will you allow me to go with you to the appointment?"

"Saxon!" She threw up her hands. "Not unless you want to make this as hard on me as possible. I know you've been away from here a long time. This is still old-fashioned Snowy Owl Crossing, where people still whisper about shotgun weddings. Please give me a few months to become the object of gossip."

"When do you plan to muzzle Doreen Mercer? I'd say she already let the cat out of the bag by telling my uncle."

"Yeah, that's a problem. She's appointed herself his BFF. I mean, she has been the most concerned about his health, to the point of delivering him healthy meals. I need to phone her." Jewell climbed out of the pickup.

"Out of curiosity," he said, matching his longer stride to her shorter one as they headed toward the entrance, "how long do you imagine you can keep it secret? Won't it soon be obvious?"

She made a face at him. "You accused me of having

time to dwell on my condition. The truth is I haven't had all that much time to get used to being pregnant. It was only after Myra commented on being happy to have gotten past morning sickness that I started to wonder. Things she described set off warning bells. I swear, Saxon, like you almost said in Leland's hospital room—we used protection. Any suspicion I might be pregnant wasn't on my radar."

"Promise you'll contact me once you see the doctor," he murmured, setting a hand on her waist as they entered the hospital.

"Okay. Can we drop the subject now?"

He didn't look happy but conceded with a nod. Increasing the pressure of his hand at the small of her back, he guided her to the elevator.

His touch, however slight, never failed to send warm tingles over Jewell's skin. She couldn't stop picturing what it'd be like if she and Saxon weren't destined to journey along paths that didn't intersect. Because the image of a life with Saxon, like his touch, left her heart unruly.

Chapter Nine

Needing to put some distance between herself and Saxon, Jewell stopped short of the elevator. "Saxon, you go on up. I really need to call Doreen. Then I'll be along."

"I thought you were too peeved with her to talk?"

"I'm over my mad. She's Lila's mom, and Lila's my best friend. Doreen did sound frantic about Leland."

"Okay. I'll stop on four and make sure he's gone off to surgery."

Jewell walked over to an empty chair near tall windows in the lobby and punched in the number for the café.

Doreen answered, sounding rushed.

"Hi, it's Jewell. I got your message. I'm back at the hospital. Leland should be going into surgery soon for a heart-valve replacement. The doctor acts as if it's fairly routine and Leland will do well."

"Heavenly days. Thank you for letting me know. From the time Porter came in blabbing about how you'd called the EMTs to Leland's ranch, I've been a basket case."

"Uh, Doreen, speaking of blabbing… I'm not happy that you overheard my private conversation with Myra the day of Lila's wedding. I'm less pleased that you told Leland."

With no hesitation the older woman apologized. "Honey, I'm sorry. Leland seemed so down when I stopped at his ranch with wedding leftovers. He fussed around, positive he'd never see Saxon again even though I said he was coming to do a benefit concert. I thought if he knew you were going to have his nephew's baby, it'd cheer him. Give him hope, you know? I swear on a stack of Bibles, I haven't told another soul."

"Please don't. Did Porter mention Saxon's already in town? He arrived early for the benefit. It's good he did. His CPR likely saved Leland. But at the hospital, Leland brought up the baby. I hadn't told Saxon, so that caused me a hugely awkward moment."

"Dear, I feel dreadful about letting the cat out of the bag. Can you ever forgive me? Oh, I hate to cut short our call, but Becky has three orders. Will you let me know how Leland's surgery goes? And truly…I'm sorry."

"I'll call, but it may be late. I'd appreciate it if you keep my secret from the other Artsy Ladies for now, too. I want to wait and tell them all together after Lila gets back."

"Understood. Mercy, if I can help you in any way, I will. Take care, you hear?"

Jewell put her phone on vibrate and caught the elevator going up.

Saxon met her outside the waiting room. "Dr. Hamlin let me see Leland before they wheeled him into the operating room. He'd had a sedative. Again he thought I was my mother. That's eerie. I only have sketchy memories of her. There must be a really strong resemblance, but…" He broke off and shook his head ruefully.

"Saxon, it's plain he really loved her."

"I'm only trying to make sense of family history I never knew. I was torn up at the time my parents were killed. But you know that since we met shortly after a caseworker located my uncle. We lived in a house in California. My folks must not have owned it. But surely there were family possessions. I only recall arriving here with a suitcase of clothes, a train set and a box of Legos. My case was handled in family court. Someone, maybe a lawyer, arranged my travel. Speaking of lawyers, Leland was still muttering about changing his will."

"That's the sedative talking, Saxon. Are you nervous? Why are you pacing out here in the hall? Let's go sit."

"Okay. I am nervous. However late I've come to recognize it, Leland's the only relative I have left. And they're operating on his heart."

"Of course. I don't know what to say other than Dr. Hamlin seemed confident the surgery will go well." Jewell felt guilty for not showing more care for Saxon's plight. She slid her arm through his but tried to let go after they found seats next to each other.

Saxon maintained his hold, threading their fingers together.

The room was quiet. One other man sat in the opposite corner drinking coffee. They drifted into silence, too.

SOON SAXON FELT Jewell's head on his shoulder and he realized she'd fallen asleep. He liked the feel of her slight weight but had to wonder if the other room occupant had seen him smile goofily down at her. Why she fought so hard against their obvious attraction escaped him. *Love.* Why couldn't he call it what it was? It was hard to recall a time he hadn't loved her. Maybe his love had flamed out after he moved to Nashville. It sure rekindled fast and hot the instant he saw her in Maryland. He'd known, of course, that no other woman he'd dated had measured up to Jewell. Or maybe he hadn't known but the feeling had been there, buried deep.

Her every glance, every touch had said she'd felt it, too.

Wasn't that proof their feelings for each other, their attachment, had never completely died? It seemed so to him. But could he make her admit they needed to raise the child they'd created together?

He felt on shaky ground and shifted his shoulder so her neck wasn't so bent.

Her hair tickled the side of his neck. Should he explain how he'd tried dating women over the years simply out of loneliness? None had filled the perpetually empty void in his life like Jewell had. Did she not see it? Maybe not. Since hurtling back into his life, she continually tried pushing him away.

Saxon's left shoulder and arm were numb from the

deadweight of his sleeping companion when Dr. Hamlin, still wearing scrubs and blue booties over his shoes, breezed in. He bolted upright quickly in anticipation of hearing what the doctor had to say, and the sudden move jarred Jewell awake.

Hamlin swung a chair around and sat. “It took three hours, but the surgery went well. Considering he’s almost seventy, and given how long he’s ignored this problem, his arteries and veins looked pretty damned good. He’ll be in recovery another hour or so and will return to ICU for a few days before I transfer him to a ward. From there his speed of recovery will dictate when I send him home.”

Jewell yawned and rubbed her eyes. “Why ICU again?”

“For closer monitoring. It’s standard after heart surgery. If recovery proceeds as I expect, he’ll spend three days there and another two or three on the surgical ward.”

“Can we see him again tonight?” Saxon asked.

“Just you. And only long enough for him to see you waited. During his sedative babbles, he expressed concern that you’d leave town and we’d relegate him to the hated rehab facility. I’m new here, but I intend to investigate the two places routinely used. Members of a community need to have confidence in their follow-up care.”

“I said I’d stay and I will. I didn’t see a cell phone in his room or I’d program in my private number.”

“He’s old-school,” Jewell murmured. “He has a house phone but no cell.”

The doctor accepted her explanation. “Are you staying at his ranch?" he asked Saxon. "I have that phone number. It's on his chart, too."

"I hate to barge into his house until he's there. I… uh…may see about a motel. Or, Jewell, didn't you say Lila owns a B and B?"

"She does, but she's on her honeymoon for two more days. I have Leland's house key. Remember, I locked up when we left."

Saxon frowned. "I'll think about staying there."

"If not, give your contact number to the staff at the ICU nursing station," Hamlin said. "I never plan on problems. Occasionally they arise. Well, I missed supper, so I want to run downstairs and grab something before I dictate his operative report."

"If I can't visit Leland tonight, I'll go on home," Jewell said, rising herself as the doctor restored his chair and left the room. "Saxon, tell Leland I'll check on him tomorrow."

"Okay. Hold on, though." He snagged her hand. "I know it's asking a lot since you're exhausted, but I'll stay at the ranch if you let me in and go in with me to see what's what."

Jewell bit her lip and rubbed her temples.

"Uh… I know you're tired, and I know you're avoiding coffee, so you wouldn't stop for that reason. The truth is I don't want to go inside and find my old bedroom has become a storage room. I wouldn't expect you to stay long, although he used to always stock soda and milk. Neither one of us finished our food in the cafeteria. It shouldn't take long to fix something. Please. What do you say?" He smiled a coaxing smile.

Jewell pursed her lips. “Okay. But… Oh, never mind. I’m sorry I used you as a pillow.”

“I’m not. I’ll offer my shoulder anytime.”

“Stop it, Saxon. We need to keep our distance. Otherwise I’m not going to go with you to Leland’s ranch.”

Saxon rubbed his shoulder as it was getting its feeling back. Biting down on all he wanted to say, he simply nodded.

Another surgeon came in and spoke to the other man who’d been waiting. They went out together, leaving Jewell and Saxon alone.

She fidgeted. “How long, do you suppose, before Leland’s out of recovery? Should you tell someone in ICU that Dr. Hamlin said you could visit him for a minute?”

“Hamlin said an hour or so. I saw a row of chairs outside the ICU. We can go down there and I’ll check in. That way we’ll be close if he comes back early.”

Jewell was at the door by the time he finished speaking. “Since you have to wait a while yet, I’ll go down to the lobby and make some phone calls. I didn’t get back with Tawana. I promised Doreen to call her after the surgery. And I should touch base with the others in my group. They’ve probably heard you’re in town. Gossip travels fast.”

“Does it matter who all knows? I want to keep a low profile.”

“Well, you’ll want to see the setup at the Grange Hall. There’s a small, movable stage. The Cattlemen’s Association frequently books live bands to play for dances, but you may need more speakers. You can reconfigure what we tentatively laid out. With Leland in the hospital, feel free to arrange taking a gander at the facility whenever it's most convenient for you. I'll see who has the key."

"That works for me. Does the high school have any small instrumental groups who play country or country rock?" he asked as this time they took the stairs. "I thought if they do, maybe a few kids would be interested in playing backup for me."

"Saxon, that's brilliant. I remember how you and a couple of other guys who played banjo and fiddle had to search for opportunities. I know the high school principal. I can give him a call, or you could run by and see the music teacher. School doesn't start until after Labor Day, but staff goes in early."

"Thanks, Jewell. You always came up with something. If you hadn't found gigs for Toby, Colton and me, I wouldn't be where I am today. I haven't thought about those dudes in years. Are they still around? Do they still play?"

Her face fell. "I'm sorry to say Colton joined the army and he died in Iraq. Toby's a calf roper. He's usually off at some rodeo."

"Now I wish even more that I hadn't let your mother steer me away from staying in contact with you. I was raised here. You gave me my country roots. Dang it all, I have too many chunks gone out of my life."

He sounded dispirited, leaving her at a loss as to what to say. Offering a quivery smile, she fell back on something she told herself to remind her why she couldn't have her work in Snowy Owl Crossing and Saxon, too.

"Things happen for a reason, Saxon. We both have the careers we always wanted."

"Yeah." He hooked his thumbs in his back pockets.

It wasn't lost on Jewell that he'd said that without enthusiasm. And when he abruptly excused himself, saying, "I'll stop here on four and meet you in the lobby later." Jewell worried that her casual comment had hurt him. That was the last thing she wanted to do. Unfortunately, a core piece of her heart would always belong to him.

ABOUT ONE HOUR LATER she spotted Saxon exiting the stairwell. His timing was perfect; she'd just signed off her last call. Her friends were sorry about Leland but happy and relieved to hear that Saxon was in town. Tawana had more questions than the others because of the rumors she'd heard on the radio. Far from ready to admit she was the old girlfriend being mentioned, Jewell did admit she was aware Saxon was taking extra time off to write new songs and, in so doing, planned to stay and help Leland after he left the hospital. If Tawana's favorite country radio station dug deeper and found her name or anything, she'd let Saxon have his people squelch that.

"Hi," she said, standing to pocket her phone when Saxon approached. "Did you see him? How is he?"

"Groggy. But he looked at me. I said you had a key to his house, and if it was okay with him, I'd stay there. He tried to squeeze my hand. But by the time I explained I'd bring him a cell phone tomorrow so he could call me whenever he wanted, he was off to la-la land. So I told a nurse that came in."

"I've never been around anyone who's had heart surgery, but I imagine they'll keep him pretty sedated for a day or so. Although they get people up fast these days. As his only relative, you're probably the only one who can visit while he's in intensive care. You'll have to keep me informed. I'll go back to my regular work schedule tomorrow unless you need me for anything."

"You're still going to call for a doctor's appointment for yourself, right?"

"Yes. Shall we head out now instead of standing here discussing stuff we can cover at Leland's house?"

Saxon's response was to pull out keys to his rental vehicle and place a hand on her back as they walked out into a balmy night.

As he'd done on the drive to the hospital, he followed her, staying a discreet distance behind her on the highway. She was grateful not to be blinded by his headlights in her mirrors. But by the time they'd reached Leland's lane, she felt so weary she wished she hadn't promised to make this side trip.

In fact, she couldn't stop yawning and her stomach felt queasy again as she climbed out of her pickup and passed Saxon the door key.

"Are you okay?" he asked when she hung back. He ran a hand up her arm after he'd turned the interior and porch lights on.

Jewell pulled away. "It's been a long day, and maybe the emptiness of this house makes me sad and weary." She took a deep breath. "Okay, let's make sure you have a bed made up to sleep in. If you want coffee, you can fix it after I leave. I don't want anything to eat or drink. I'm anxious to get home to bed."

"All right. I'll bring in my duffel and guitars later. So many of our shows start at nine p.m., I'm pretty much a night owl."

That comment made Jewell smile. "You're the antithesis of our snowies, then," she joked, laughing outright when he made a face at her. "We see them out and about at all daylight hours."

Because they both knew where his old bedroom was in the house, they went straight down the hall.

"Hey," Saxon exclaimed. "Can you believe the room is the same as when I came by after college graduation to collect my personal stuff?"

"This is the desk where you used to study. Wow, it's like stepping back in time. Those posters of country stars you put up in high school are out-of-date now."

"Yeah. Roy Clark, who used to be the guitar sensation, has been replaced by Keith Urban. I saw the Oak Ridge Boys a year or so ago when they performed for someone receiving an award at the Kennedy Center. Some of these others are over-the-hill. I shouldn't say that. The other day Donovan reminded me there are young guys nipping at my heels."

"At thirty-one?" She gave a half laugh. "This is new," she said, running a hand over the bedspread.

"The bed is different, too. I had a twin. This one's bigger. Do you think he used it as a guest room?"

She shrugged. "Maybe, but he never mentioned visitors. We know you're his only relative. To my knowledge, until this year when he arranged for Eddie Four Bear and Aaron Younger to work his fields, he never hired helpers."

"It doesn't matter," Saxon said. "I'm grateful to have a bigger bed."

"Doesn't surprise me considering the bed in your bus is huge." Suddenly her mentioning the bed where they'd spent stormy hours making love in the not-too-distant past caused her to blush and stammer out, "C-can we g-go out now? If we're finished, I'll head home."

"Help me check the kitchen. I need to know if there's stuff for breakfast or if I need to go to the café in the morning."

Saxon turned on the kitchen light and went straight to the cupboard that held the coffee.

Jewell watched him dump stale coffee from the pot—probably left over from Leland's breakfast. She peered in the fridge while he measured new grounds. "You coming back here after so long is a lot like what people say about riding a bicycle—you don't forget. It shows what creatures of habit we are. Leland's coffee is stored in the same spot it was when you were young. My kitchen is still set up like my mom had it."

"Amazing. I didn't have to hunt for grounds or a mug." He held one up to prove his point.

The coffee soon began to perk and Jewell wrinkled her nose. "Yuck, coffee smell is one thing that plays havoc with my stomach." She opened the freezer door. "But look, he wasn't kidding about the juice can with the key to his desk drawer being in the freezer." She held it out and scraped off a layer of frost. "I'm not surprised he forgot about the insurance policies. This can has about twenty years of frost on it. And I found it behind a package of beef that has freezer burn and should be tossed out."

"Put the can back. I'll let him get out those policies." Saxon stopped to inspect an old wall phone. "This is a relic. I wonder if he'd use a cell if I buy one and prepay for minutes. This phone doesn't even have an answering machine." Saxon lifted the receiver. "There is a dial tone."

Jewell had stopped at the kitchen table and was looking at a notepad lying there. She let out a gasp that had Saxon whirling around.

"What's wrong?" He returned the receiver to its cradle and joined her.

"He really was thinking about altering his will before his collapse. When I stopped here this morning, he asked me in, saying there was something he wanted to talk about. This note mentions leaving his ranch to our baby." She crumpled the page. "As his only blood relative, you should inherit his property."

Saxon lightly scraped his fingers down her cheek. "It's his decision, Jewell. Technically, any child of mine is his blood relative."

"But...but...he shouldn't cut you out," she sputtered. "That's not right."

"I've never expected anything from him. I don't need anything."

Jewell flipped the page and saw writing on the one below. "Saxon, look at this. He's proposing to...oh, make it so our group can't buy his forest for our owls." She let the pad drop.

Saxon scooped it up. "Ah, I see what's got your goat. He thinks this will manipulate us into marriage."

Jewell crossed her arms and locked her hands around her elbows. "It's just wrong."

Saxon took her fully in his arms. "This may be something he considered, sweetheart, but he hasn't spoken to Weiss."

"I'm not your sweetheart, Saxon. Why would he meddle like this?"

"I guess he doesn't want the Conrad name to end with me. And you said some folks here still believe in shotgun weddings. Just so we're crystal clear…from my perspective, I have every intention of coparenting our child."

She was near enough to inhale his cologne, and a big part of Jewell wanted to remain wrapped in his embrace. A smaller part urged her to object. She might have done so, except Saxon's cell phone chimed.

Jewell could tell the way he released her and fumbled for the instrument that he, like she, worried that the call could be about Leland.

Thankfully, she saw his tight jaw relax. "Sid. I know it's late in Nashville, but I need to return your call. My uncle's had emergency heart surgery. He came through all right, but frankly, it's been a rough few hours."

Fully disengaging from the arm Saxon still had around her, Jewell claimed his attention with a dismissive wave and started to walk away.

He tugged her back. His explosive retort to his caller had her stopping to listen.

"I don't give a damn what Fred wants. We agreed I'd get time off to write. I intend to do that and assist my uncle once he's released from the hospital. Don't set me up to perform next week in Boise and Great Falls. I mean it, Sid. Tell Fred no, or I'll be a no-show." He clicked off and slammed the phone down so hard the kitchen table rocked.

His hand dropped from Jewell's back. In a strained voice, he said, "I'm upset. You're tired. And it's ten o'clock. It's probably best if we hold off discussing this further tonight. Let's wait until after you see the doctor. I'll talk to Leland when he's up to it. God knows I already have enough people meddling in my life. In a sense, though, I agree with him. I want our baby to have my name, Jewell."

Making a garbled sound in her throat, she dashed from the room.

Saxon raced after her—all the way to where she slammed out the front door. The old door stuck. He had to yank on it several times for it to open. When he stepped on the porch, Jewell was already firing up her pickup.

He watched her back in a semicircle and drive off. He spent a breathless moment considering whether or not to follow. But she wasn't driving too fast, and she lived less than a quarter mile away.

Rubbing the furrows carved between his eyebrows, he decided it was probably better to give her space. No doubt his uncle thought he'd be doing Jewell a favor. It'd be natural for a man who judged Saxon as having run away from family to make his mark in Nashville to believe he might balk rather than man up and do his duty.

His uncle was of a generation who'd expect them to marry and raise their child together. He wanted that, too. But Jewell acted as if she wasn't open to even coparenting. She'd made it clear that she assumed he'd leave after the benefit, which meant what? His only having spotty visitations? Oh, yeah, he'd seen her eyes narrow as she listened to him talk to Sid about future performances. Of course, he knew their reason for wanting him to go on the road again so soon was tied to the possible CMA Entertainer of the Year nomination.

Feeling caught between a rock and a hard place, Saxon went back inside to drink that coffee and sit down to mull over what he could do to appease everyone and keep juggling all the balls in the air.

Chapter Ten

Driving home, Jewell's brain was in total turmoil. Maybe hearing she was pregnant with Saxon's baby had made Leland go a little nuts. Did he really presume he could play matchmaker? Everyone in town knew her group wanted his timber for a snowy owl refuge, so possibly he did.

After parking and letting herself into the house, she was greeted by two dogs delighted to see her. However, totally tuckered out, she went directly to bed and didn't object when a dog snuggled in on each side of her. It was comforting even if right before she fell asleep, she felt like the filling in a pet sandwich.

THE NEXT MORNING Jewell took a call from a rancher with sick steers. They arranged to meet at his pasture, and she looked up the number for Myra's OB. On her way to the ranch, she called for an appointment. She expected it'd be a week or more to get in, but the receptionist said, "You're in luck. My last phone call was a cancellation for tomorrow at one. Can you come then?"

Of course she could. She confirmed the time, trying

not to think about Saxon asking to go along. His request was never far from her thoughts, however. Truthfully, she wasn't ready for that level of involvement. Not yet, and possibly not ever, under the circumstances.

Once she'd dispensed medication to the sick cattle, she phoned Saxon to see if he'd seen Leland. Her call went to his voice mail. Rather than leave a message, she contacted the ICU desk. The nurse remembered her and said, "Mr. Conrad had a good night. His nephew was by earlier. I see Dr. Hamlin has limited visitations to immediate family until he's moved to a ward."

Jewell thanked her and went to her clinic to meet a neighbor with a sick puppy. Her day became a series of callouts. Saxon left her a message that Leland looked okay but was too groggy to talk. Since Saxon wasn't spending the day at the hospital, she wondered what he was doing with his first free day back in town.

The following morning another rancher phoned. "I'm worried my milk cows ate bitterweed I found in my pasture, Jewell."

Once she explained he wasn't the first in the area to find the weed, he promised to notify the Cattlemen's Association so everyone could get together and spray.

The hours passed quickly. All too soon she faced going to see the OB. Being in medicine herself, she shouldn't have been so nervous. After all, she helped deliver cows, horses, sheep, dogs and cats. Maybe because she'd run into some tough problems, that caused her anxiety.

As she hurried home to shower off the cattle smell, her cell rang. Caller ID indicated it was Saxon. Rather than take his call, she opted to wait until after her appointment. Otherwise he'd pressure her to let him go along. Really, she'd only promised to relay what the doctor said.

Later, at the clinic, she was ushered into a room and given a gown. A chatty nurse weighed and measured her and logged her vitals. Soon the doctor, young, pretty and personable, whisked into the room. She set Jewell at ease, even during the invasive check no woman liked.

"I estimate you're eight or nine weeks pregnant," Dr. Archer announced after helping Jewell sit up.

"Eight," Jewell responded, and haltingly explained how she could be so sure right down to the day of conception. "Also, my periods are erratic. I didn't realize I'd missed one until the friend who referred me, who'd gone through morning sickness, made me suspicious of my symptoms. I'm not only queasy and dizzy in the morning. Is that normal?"

The doctor smiled. "Yes. But take prenatal vitamins. If, as you say, you've lost weight, drink this supplement." She wrote on a prescription pad. "Given your occupation, in another couple of months you should wear a maternity support belt. About your symptoms. There are no absolute norms. With luck your discomfort will abate by the time I see you for your first ultrasound. Um, I see you're single. Do you have concerns about going through this alone?"

"No. Yes. I don't know."

The doctor smiled. "That's a normal reaction. Remember, I'm available to answer questions, and no question is too inconsequential. If you haven't told the father, my advice would be to get that over with. However, it's totally up to you."

"He knows. He's in town temporarily."

"Ah, military or rodeo cowboy?"

"Neither. But I promised to tell him how I am. Is it okay if he wants to come to my appointments?"

"If he cares, that's good. I've no objection if you wish to include him at your ultrasound. Some non-husbands fade away once they've seen the tangible evidence. Some see the fetus and are moved to commit."

"Hmm. I'll consider it if he's still in town."

Dr. Archer accepted that and directed Jewell out to speak with the receptionist.

She booked her next visit and left the clinic mulling over what the doctor had said. Saxon thought he wanted to be involved. The doctor sounded as if she thought witnessing the ultrasound might change his mind. Rather than phone him with results, Jewell elected to run by Leland's ranch to see if she could catch him. He could be there writing songs.

When she pulled into the yard, his vehicle was parked at the house.

She reached the porch and remembered the panic she'd gone through seeing Leland collapse there. Would she ever come here again without picturing it? She started to knock, then heard loud sounds coming from out back.

She reversed course, rounded the house and saw Saxon, shirtless, splitting wood. His back muscles bunched each time he swung the ax, and his skin glistened with sweat. It shocked her to see him doing physical labor. He'd never wanted to help around the ranch. But shock wasn't all she felt. Desire gnawed at her enough to have her clutching her stomach.

Moving nearer, she swallowed and yelled, "Saxon, what in heaven's name are you doing?" She actually feared he'd cut off his left hand the way he stood a piece of wood on a stump and brought the gleaming ax down through it.

Pausing, he spun, saw her and grinned. "I'm cutting wood. What does it look like I'm doing?"

"Why?" Jewell waved a hand aimlessly, more to cool her face than anything.

"Eddie Four Bear said the temperature's gonna dip, and it might rain. I remembered Leland liked sitting by his fireplace. I figured I'd fill the shed near the house with wood so he can have fires after he gets out of the hospital. I left you a message earlier."

"I had a doctor's appointment."

"You did? How did that go?" He buried the blade in the stump, then reached for a T-shirt and rubbed it down his chest.

Jewell's eyes tracked the path of the soft fabric before she blurted, "I'm pregnant. Eight weeks."

"And...?"

"I'm otherwise healthy."

"Great. Is there more?"

"Next visit I'll have an ultrasound and you can go if you'd like." Her words ran together in her nervousness.

"I would like. I'll get the date and time later. I want to finish this stack and go see Leland before I meet a trio of high schoolers for a jam session in one kid's barn. He plays drums, another the keyboard, and a third a steel guitar. The high school music teacher rounded them all up. I'm flattered to know they play some of my songs. They'll be great backup at the benefit."

"The useless benefit since Leland won't sell us his trees unless you and I…uh…commit to the impossible."

"Patience, Jewell. Let him heal. Then we'll see."

"I have an hour before someone brings a pup in to be neutered. Oh, but you want to finish cutting wood. I thought maybe I could show you the Grange Hall."

"Tawana and Hunter took me to see it. I ate breakfast at the café, and Doreen introduced us. She's anxious for news of Leland. Are those two more than friends? She knew what microwave meals are in his freezer."

"Huh? I'm stuck back on Tawana and Hunter taking you to the Grange."

"Yeah. The layout you ladies planned is perfect. Do you know the concert has sold out? Tawana asked if I'd donate some CDs for a raffle at your bazaar. I gave her T-shirts, too."

"Wow, you've made yourself right at home with my friends," she said huffily.

"Better get used to it. I said I plan to stick around. I also met the newlyweds and Lila's son. Lila seems happy." He tossed his T-shirt aside, yanked the ax out of the stump and, turning his back on Jewell, cut the next piece of wood into kindling.

She winced at each swing. Deciding he did know how to handle an ax but unwilling to disturb him again to apologize for her snarkiness, she returned to her pickup. She didn't like being bitchy. Saxon was doing something nice for Leland, and the Owl Café served as a hub in town where everyone met. Plus he'd gone to school with Lila, like she had.

Maybe part of her reaction had been hearing him say Lila and Seth were back. With Myra, Doreen, Saxon and the OB doc all knowing her condition, it meant she couldn't hold off much longer from telling her other friends she was pregnant. She worried that they, too, might try to pressure her into marriage. So, confessing wasn't made easier having Saxon in town. Exactly what had he meant when he said he planned to stick around? Stick around for how long after the doctor cleared Leland for normal activity? Saxon's life was on the road.

As she neared her clinic, it struck her that she'd never felt this conflicted about anything in her life. Well, maybe the first time she'd let Saxon go his way while she went hers. Now was different. It wasn't only the two of them his leaving would affect—there was the child they'd made together. Dads were important.

But so were lifelong careers.

If only Leland hadn't needed to contact him. Eventually, she surely would have gotten past admitting some part of her had always longed to be Mrs. Saxon Conrad.

THE OWNER OF the pup needing surgery drove in behind her. Jewell parked, hopped out and wiped personal thoughts from her head. She went into professional vet mode and performed the surgery.

Sometime afterward, she made a conscious decision to wait until after Saxon's concert to come clean with the rest of her friends. She'd bury herself in work and avoid everyone, which wasn't abnormal for her.

Except that she had Lila's dog. Quickly she left a message on the B-and-B phone asking to keep Ghost a few more weeks. She pleaded busyness and that Ghost was a settling influence on Shadow. That part was true, anyway.

The next day the weather took a downswing. Some range cattle didn't fare well in the unexpected freeze. It kept Jewell busy at outlying ranches.

Most nights that week she came home beat and with barely enough energy to feed the animals and herself. It was good she hadn't needed to fib to her friends.

Saxon left a string of messages on her cell and home phones throughout the next two weeks. She didn't return his calls. Partly because she was gone from dawn to after dark, but also because she needed longer to build up inner reserves to see him again. Luckily, she heard via the grapevine that Leland was doing well enough to be discharged the day after the concert, which meant Saxon would be tied down thereafter himself. Just two more days and they'd see each other at the concert.

HOSPITAL STAFF HAD moved Leland into a two-bed ward. His roommate had gone home, and now Saxon steered his uncle back from a walk down the hall.

"I'm feeling gobs better. I'm ready to go home," the old man said, nevertheless accepting help swinging his feet back up onto his bed. "Surprises me how many people have come to see me. Not Jewell, although she calls."

"I haven't said anything, but she saw a note on your

kitchen table that upset her. Do you remember writing out a plan to exchange letting her group buy your timber only if we legally give the baby our last name?"

"More'n that! Jewell deserves a husband," he said gruffly. "When Doreen first told me Jewell had come back in the family way from a mission I sent her on, I felt awful. Then Doreen said you were coming here to give a concert. Knowing Jewell loves those owls, and you, I hatched a plan to nudge you two knuckleheads a bit. Just what are your intentions, boy?"

Taken aback, Saxon said nothing, but sat, hands clasped between his knees.

"No doubt you see me as a meddling old fool. Truth is, I let losing Bernadette turn me into a bitter man. I don't know what happened between you and Jewell. It doesn't take a genius to see how things stand. You want her. She wants you. You've made a baby, but something's keeping you apart. Shouldn't you rectify that?"

"I don't know how. Her life is here. Mine's not."

"You saying you can't live here and be a singer?"

Tension gripped Saxon's body. "I appreciate what you're saying. It might help if you'd tell her you won't be tying that timber up in your will. No matter how well intentioned, Uncle Leland, you can't fix Jewell's and my differences."

"Here's the last thing I'll say on the subject. It takes two to mend fences."

Saxon nodded, but something told him that wasn't true. As a kid living here, hadn't he seen many a rancher stringing fence wire alone? Still, the whole conversation gave him a lot to mull over.

At 10:00 p.m. the night before the show, Jewell again crawled into bed between two dogs. Cold as it had been out at a ranch on a windswept day, she let their warmth lull her to sleep almost as soon as her head touched the pillow.

All at once she was awakened by someone pounding on her kitchen door. Both dogs leaped off the bed and set up a ruckus. Afraid someone had an animal with a terrible emergency, Jewell pulled on her boots and grabbed her robe. "Shush," she told the dogs, and went to open the door a crack to keep Shadow and Ghost from attacking whoever was outside. It shocked her to see Saxon, his arm raised to knock again.

"Why haven't you returned my calls?" he demanded. He narrowed his eyes. "Are you sick? Is there something wrong with the baby? You don't look so good." Barging in, he wrapped her in his arms and pressed a kiss to her forehead.

"Just what a woman wants to hear in the middle of the night. I'm fine. I've had an overly full schedule with crazy hours. You woke me. I was in bed asleep."

He pulled back, kicked the door shut with a heel but looked sheepish. "Sorry. My schedule's been nuts, too. Mornings I compose, noon I visit Leland, afternoons I've been cleaning the house of dust, cobwebs and old newspapers. Evenings I jam with the high school kids. I drive past here most nights, but your lights have been out. Tonight there was one on in your kitchen, so I stopped."

Jewell scrunched the collar of her robe under her chin. "I must've forgotten to shut it off." She spoke to the top of his head, because he'd bent to pet the dogs. "Is everything set for the benefit? I admit I've avoided calling any of the Artsy Ladies to hold off telling them about the baby."

"Why?"

"They'll cluck over me, and I hate being clucked over."

Straightening, he laughed. "I don't know what that means exactly. I've met all of your group. None strike me as women who'd like being compared to hens."

"You're right. Please don't tell them what I said, or even that I've dodged them on purpose. How is Leland? I've only talked to him by phone. Today he volunteered that he's not messing with his will. Is that true, and is he really being discharged day after tomorrow?"

"That's the plan. So I told him you'd seen his note and were upset. Maybe I should've left it to you, but I took the opportunity when it came up."

"Thank you for that. Frankly, I didn't say anything, not knowing how fragile his heart is."

"He claims he has more pep than he has had in years. Hey, I'd better go and let you get back to bed. You'll be at my concert, right?"

"Yes. I'm slated to usher. If you see Lila tomorrow, tell her I'll be there. Oh, but wait, hasn't she stopped working the breakfast shift at the café?"

"She's training a friend of Tawana's. Yesterday she asked if I'd seen you. She said you left her a cryptic message about keeping Rory's dog until after the concert, because he settles Shadow." Saxon studied the animals who both sat wagging their tails. “They’re a pair, aren’t they?”

“Yeah. I worried Lila would come after Ghost and guilt would’ve made me tell her my news before the others. I promised Myra and Doreen I’d update everyone after the concert. Myra said it’s hard to keep quiet, and it’s killing Doreen.”

“I still don’t get why it’s so hard to tell all of your friends.”

“To take the heat off you, Saxon. With Leland coming home, you can stay out of their reach. Even if I accept total blame, Lila and Tawana will hold you responsible. I didn’t want you to have to deal with their barbs before your show. I mean, we invited you. They shouldn’t give you flak, but my best friends will. I’ll hate that. Do you want coffee?” she asked out of the blue.

Saxon rubbed the back of his neck. “I’m trying to process all you said. We should just tell them together.”

“I can’t!” She went to the kitchen counter and got down the coffee can.

“Stop. I don’t need coffee this late, and the smell makes you sick.”

“Actually, I’m past that little evil. Out on the range coffee flows. Today the smell didn’t bother me. But you’re right—it’s late and I have a day’s work tomorrow at a sheep ranch. I hope I’m finished in time to feed the dogs, shower and change for the concert.”

He walked to the door but turned and frowned. “You’d better not skip out, Jewell. We won’t start until I see you.”

"How you talk. I look forward to seeing a whole performance without worry of a hurricane or a blizzard. The almanac says our first freeze is behind us. There won't be another until nearer Thanksgiving." She grabbed the dogs' collars. "I'll hold these guys so they don't race out with you."

Saxon went back to her, tipped up her chin and kissed her squarely on the lips. He didn't rush the kiss, either. When he eased back, he smiled down into her confused eyes. "I couldn't resist, since you were captive." He left then with a jaunty spring in his step. "Lock up," he called. "And turn off your kitchen lights this time."

Jewell let go of the dogs but felt herself smile because it wasn't a hardship to return to bed with the taste of Saxon on her lips. If only… Hugging Shadow, she didn't let herself finish that thought.

STARTING EARLY THE next morning Jewell checked a sheep owner's animals for sores and ear mites after he ran each one through sheep dip. It was a dirty, smelly job, and she was so thankful her queasiness had passed.

The rancher owned a huge flock. They barely finished at the last possible time she'd set for getting home to ready herself for the concert.

While her morning sickness had gone, the tiredness remained. She'd lifted a plethora of squirming lambs who'd tried desperately to escape the spray. Now her back ached from shoulders to thighs. Letting hot water beat on her lower back, Jewell wondered if she should already be wearing a maternity belt. The doctor had said to call if she had questions. She might do that.

PEOPLE WERE LINED up to get inside the hall when Jewell drove in and had to circle the building to find parking. The side door was closer, but it was locked. She knocked, hoping to attract someone's attention. A teen dressed in fancy Western wear opened the door. "You can't come in this way," he said and started to shut it again.

Jewell stuck her foot in the opening. "I'm a worker bee. Part of the group who arranged for this show. Who are you?"

"A member of Mr. Conrad's band," he mumbled, casting a nervous glance around. "The lady out front said she'd have our heads if we let people in the side doors. I shouldn't have answered your knock."

Jewell spotted Saxon wending his way to the makeshift stage. He looked so handsome she felt the beat of her heart in her ears. She was barely able to call out to him. He set down his guitar case and rushed over.

"Hey, you made it. Myra and Tawana are up front fending off fans who tried to waylay me for autographs. Lila's helping her mom ready soft drinks and cookies by the far wall." He pointed. "I asked all of them if they'd seen you. When no one had, frankly, we were all worried. Why are you standing outside? Royce, let her in," he told the kid.

"Yes, sir, Mr. Conrad. Ms. Tawana said not to let anyone in a side door."

"Jewell's special. Hey, I thought I told you kids to call me Saxon. I know you think I'm old, but don't make me feel older." He chuckled to show there was no sting in his mild rebuke.

Jewell stepped in and yanked the door until the automatic lock clicked. "I'd better go let the others know I'm here to help seat folks."

Smiling, he ran his gaze over her skinny black jeans and orange blouse. "You look amazing," he said, fingering the tail of her lone braid. "That color brings out golden fire in your red hair. Incidentally, no one will believe you're pregnant," he murmured for Jewell's ears alone.

His possessive stance and tone had Jewell tingling with desire for another kiss like the one he'd left her with last night. She knew she was blushing. "Doubt me if you want, but I know my body's changing. You'll see at the ultrasound."

"I don't doubt you," he said, but she'd already sped off.

"Is she your girlfriend?" asked a second teen as he came over to set up his keyboard.

"Huh?" The question jarred him out of his reverie. "We're a little old for that term to apply. But she was my girlfriend when we were your age."

"She's really pretty. Isn't she a veterinarian?"

"Correct."

"And you live in Nashville. I guess that's why she didn't stay your girlfriend."

Saxon scowled, then endeavored to smooth it away. "I'm back in town now," he said firmly enough to silence the kid's line of questions.

JEWELL STORED HER purse in a room used as a coat check in winter. She muted her cell phone and joined her friends at the entrance.

"It's about darned time you showed up," Tawana exclaimed. "Mindy and Shelley are out giving tickets for free snacks. They said we should send out a search dog."

"You all know it's my busy season," Jewell said. "Myra, you're rubbing your back. Do you need a break? Why are you guys standing instead of sitting?"

"We've had last-minute sales. Visitors in town. Our seating was at capacity for fire code. The only way we could add two more was to give up our chairs."

"I heard we were sold out."

Myra eyed Jewell. "Yesterday Zeke noticed Leland's sale sign was down. Tawana phoned you to ask if he'd sold it, but you didn't call her back. So Lila stopped at the realty office. They said he pulled his listing. Does that bode well for us to buy his forest?"

Jewell made a face. "I'll address that and other stuff later. Can we grab a few minutes together after the crowd clears, before we begin cleanup?"

From the way Myra gave her an understanding nod and squeezed her arm, Jewell knew her pregnant friend had guessed part of her news.

Tawana checked her watch. "It's time to open up and let the mob in. Seating is first come, first serve, Jewell. Some of us talked about that last week when you weren't available and didn't bother to ever get back to us." She glared a bit.

Refusing to be baited, Jewell responded. "Most days I left at dawn and got home way after dark. I didn't have time to take Rory's dog back until I dropped him off today. Don't be mad."

Her friend sighed. "I'm not. I'm sure you've been plenty rattled since you found Leland unresponsive.

Hunter says if the old guy balks at selling us the forest, you can remind him how lucky he is that you went by his house that hour of that day."

Jewell brooded a moment. Might the fact she helped save his life convince him to consider selling them his forest? Or should Saxon not have told Leland she was upset?

Hurriedly, she began directing people to rows and later ones to single empty seats. The hall filled fast. She and Shelley closed the doors.

Saxon stepped to the mike. "All right. The show will start in a matter of minutes." He introduced his backup team, and Jewell could tell the boys hadn't expected it but loved the attention.

Looking around, she saw the other Artsy Ladies had all gone to stand behind the food table with Doreen and Lila. She joined them but sat on the floor.

The first song, Saxon's latest hit, transported her back to the concert in Maryland. His deep voice sent shivers up her spine. Part of her worried he'd sing the songs written for her that she'd asked him not to. But he did a string of old favorites and she began to relax. He and the teens received numerous standing ovations. She was transported back to when they were young and in love. She found herself wishing this day would never end. She didn't want to return to the reality of their broken relationship.

"Time's flown by," Saxon announced. "The next number will be our last."

Jewell looked at her watch, disbelieving an hour and a half had passed.

"I wrote this song special for tonight," he said, and Jewell climbed awkwardly to her feet. Her stomach cramped in anticipation that he'd gone back on his word.

But the song was about providing a refuge for the snowy owls. It was funny and poignant, and the crowd loved it. They loved it more when Saxon thanked everyone for coming and, pointing to the back of the room, thanked each of the Artsy Ladies by name. "They invited me to give this benefit to raise money for an owl refuge but insisted on paying my expenses. I'm donating that money back to the cause."

Some people rushed the stage to rave about the show. Others hurried to the snack table for sodas and cookies and to applaud their group for bringing such a great show to town. Jewell tried to keep Saxon in sight, but the next twenty minutes were a flurry of activity. Soon everyone including the band and Saxon had cleared out.

Lila and Tawana danced around hugging each other.

"Time to clean up this place, but what a success," Myra exclaimed. "And isn't that great about Saxon returning his portion of the profits? Will that give us enough to make Leland an offer?"

After most responded that they didn't know, Mindy pulled out two garbage bags from a box Doreen had brought and set to raving about Saxon. "He's the hottest guy I've seen in town since the rodeo left. I can't believe you let him get away, Jewell. He could park his boots under my bed any day." She sighed and tapped her heart.

Myra shot Jewell a sidelong glance and tried to shush Mindy.

However, Jewell confronted her. "Well, Mindy, while

in Maryland I parked *my* boots beside his bed. In March I'll be having his baby."

Chatter stopped dead. Everyone but Myra and Doreen gasped. "So have you seen my OB and know for sure?" Myra broke the stunned silence.

"Yes."

A rush of questions turned into interrogations demanding of Jewell just when she planned to work in a wedding.

"Not gonna happen," she mumbled.

"May I ask why not?" Tawana burst out.

Jewell grimaced. "Suffice to say it's complicated."

"As stubbornly traditional as Leland is, he'll be unhappy," Doreen put in. "I shouldn't have told him you were pregnant, Jewell."

"I wish you hadn't. He wants the baby to carry the Conrad name."

"I know." Doreen wrung her hands. "He fretted, blaming himself for asking you to see Saxon in Maryland."

"That's silly." Jewell dismissed the notion with a flick of her wrist.

They all fussed over Jewell as she had been afraid they'd do, and also as she expected, Lila had some harsh words for Saxon.

Stacking a last set of chairs, Jewell pulled Lila aside. "Don't fault Saxon. He invited me to go along on his tour. I had my practice and the obligation to work the rodeo. Fault our circumstances. Our careers will always divide us."

"Really? I mean, you two are having a baby. That's pretty uniting."

Jewell scraped back her hair. "Is life on the road any place to raise a child?"

"Can't Saxon tour from here?" Lila asked.

"He'd be gone 70 percent of the time." Jewell slumped against the wall. "I just think that'd be so hard on our child."

"Don't you really mean it'd be hard on you to have him dash in and out of your life? I'm sorry, because you still look at him with love. Today it was written all over your face. Being a single mom for as long as I was after Keith died, even with my mother's help, I realize acutely since Seth came into our lives how much a kid benefits from having a dad around."

Jewell stared at her feet. She wanted her baby's father to be involved. "Saxon claims he wants to share parenting. I'm not sure how long that might last after he goes back to performing around the country. The other night his agent called wanting him to sing in Boise and Great Falls. Saxon had to refuse because he promised to be Leland's caregiver for a few weeks. How long do you think his label will stand for him skipping shows? Like it or not, he's a big star."

"Pfft on him, then. Your baby will be loved by five devoted aunties and a few uncles. As for the snowy refuge, if Leland won't negotiate with us, maybe Mom can talk him around. They seem to get along, and both are mulish."

"I hate to picture those two going head-to-head. But it'd be great if she could get him to sell the forest to us.

He can't sniff at the amount we've raised, and that's not counting what we'll make at the Thanksgiving bazaar."

"Exactly. Let's be positive."

Chapter Eleven

Every client Jewell saw after the concert raved about it. Those who'd missed it asked if she thought Saxon could be talked into giving another show. She'd never dreamed how difficult it'd be to keep hearing his name, but she was thankful her pregnancy remained a secret for now.

"Saxon is looking after Leland," she told Sarah Jane Watson, who, the morning Jewell answered a call at the Watson ranch, pressed her about Saxon possibly doing a Christmas show at the Cattlemen's Association's banquet. "We've only spoken on the phone since Labor Day, but unless his uncle's recovery takes longer than expected, I doubt Saxon will still be here at Christmas."

"Oh, but Royce Lambert's dad told Hank that Saxon is joining the boys for two numbers in the high school holiday show," Sarah said. "Our banquet is the following Saturday. We'd pay him, of course."

After hearing Saxon would be in town for the high school program, Jewell faltered in tending the sick colt. "I truly don't know his schedule, Sarah. Do you have Leland's home phone number?"

"Yes, but you know Saxon better than anyone. I

thought if you asked, he'd be more apt to agree. I remember you used to hunt places for him to perform."

"A long time ago." Frankly, she'd even put off seeing Leland since he came home, because she didn't want to dicker over his land. The Artsy Ladies were bugging her to ask him since no one but Tawana had much to sell at this year's bazaar.

"What if I ask Saxon to call you? I'm behind banding owl chicks. If I have a free evening, I'm trying to knit for the bazaar. It will be here before we know it."

"Just put in a good word for me."

Jewell left the Watson ranch feeling bad that she hadn't been truly forthcoming with Sarah Jane. Her ultrasound was the next day and Saxon intended to go.

IN THE MORNING she was surprised when he drove in. She thought they'd agreed to meet at the clinic.

He climbed out of his SUV. "Hi. Doreen came to the ranch to fix Leland breakfast and stay with him until I get back. She thought it'd look better if you and I went together."

Jewell frowned. "Doreen closed the café to stay with Leland?"

"No. She said the woman she hired to replace Lila is a dynamo. Doreen's been spending quite a bit of time at the ranch teaching me to make heart-healthy meals."

"No kidding? Okay, well, follow me to the clinic. I have to visit a ranch for a client when I leave there."

He seemed disappointed but climbed back in his vehicle.

At the clinic they parked side by side. "Before I forget, Sarah Jane Watson wants to talk to you about singing at the Cattlemen's Association Christmas banquet. Here, I wrote her number down. Call her if you'd like." Jewell passed him a slip of paper that he tucked in his shirt pocket.

"No problem—I can do that."

"Is Leland doing poorly? I thought he'd be on his own well before Christmas."

"He's doing great." Saxon escorted her to the door with a hand at her waist, as was normal for him.

Jewell winced, wondering if he could feel how her waist had expanded. It was barely into October, but she'd started wearing her shirts loose and unbuttoning the top button of her jeans. Nevertheless, she still liked Saxon's proprietary touch.

Inside, a nurse took Jewell to a room and gave her a gown. "I'll bring your husband back when Dr. Archer is ready to do the ultrasound."

Jewell didn't bother explaining that Saxon wasn't her husband, but the comment made her sad. She was nervous, too, about him seeing the ultrasound.

The jelly a technician spread on her stomach was cold. She felt overly exposed, too. Especially when the doctor came in chatting with Saxon.

The picture was jumpy and dark at first, then got clearer. Fascinated, Jewell tore her gaze away when Saxon clasped her hand and said, "Look, there's our baby."

After that she didn't hear much of what Dr. Archer said until she instructed the tech to print them each a copy of the screen.

Saxon continued looking awestruck. Maybe she did, too.

They sent him out to wait while she dressed.

Dr. Archer asked if Jewell had questions or was experiencing any problems. She shook her head. “Oh, wait. Do I need a prescription to buy a maternity belt?”

“No. Buy one at any pharmacy. If there’s nothing else, I’ll see you in a month. I must say, your baby’s father handled that well. You’d be surprised how many faint dead away.” Smiling, she departed. Shortly thereafter, Jewell met Saxon in the waiting room.

“You don’t need to hang around. I have to book my next appointment.”

“I’ll wait. I have something for you in my car. I can’t believe it slipped my mind. I know you’ll be pleased.”

Her curiosity piqued, Jewell made her appointment and followed him to where they’d parked.

Saxon opened his car door and brought out a sheaf of papers. “Uncle Leland had Jim Weiss drop by the ranch. This is your copy of a notarized deed to the timber. He’s giving you the land for a refuge, Jewell.”

A tremor ran through her. “Why? What’s made him change his mind?” She almost dropped the bundle. “We can pay,” she said, feeling tears trickle over her lower eyelids as she read her name on the deed. “This is too much. He’s okay, isn’t he?”

“He’s fine, but he won’t take your money.” Saxon brushed aside a lock of her hair that the wind had whipped loose from an untidy knot she’d hastily pinned up before the ultrasound.

"Feel that? It's snowing. Let's go to the café. I'm sure you'll want to tell your friends the news."

"I have a date with cattle, Saxon. Relay my gratitude. Tell Leland I'll come by soon to hug him." She rubbed at snowflakes and tears. "I'm totally blown away. Would he hate it or be pleased if we dedicate the site to him and post it as the Conrad Snowy Owl Refuge?"

"He'll probably like that. He's mellowed, Jewell. We've had some heart-to-heart talks both before and after he got out of the hospital. He's a man with a new lease on life."

"That's wonderful. Then...you'll be able to leave soon."

The flakes fell faster. Saxon slipped an arm around her, hustled her to her pickup and boosted her in out of the weather. "What do I need to do to convince you I'm not going anywhere?"

"Until after Christmas? I heard a rumor to that effect." She set the deed on the console and touched her cold fingers to his equally cold cheeks. "Where's your cowboy hat? You have snowflakes in your hair and eyelashes."

"I don't understand why you're so anxious to have me gone. It's taken a while, but I finally see there's more I want here than anywhere else," he said seriously.

"Oh, Saxon. I know you were terrifically moved by the ultrasound. I'm happy that you and Leland have made peace. Still, you're bound to grow restless in our small town or when your career tugs at you. It's okay, Saxon. Honestly."

"I discovered I like writing songs. I've sold two to

a top country artist. Love songs, Jewell. Your name isn't in them, but I wrote them for you. For you and our baby."

"Please stop! It's too much, Saxon. If this is about wanting shared custody, we can work something out."

"I want more than shared custody. Hey, it's snowing harder. Are you sure you have to go out to a cattle ranch?"

She nodded.

"Drive carefully. Call me when you get home." He closed her door gently, ducked his head and sprinted to his SUV.

Jewell started her pickup, all the while wrestling with what he'd said. What did he mean—he wanted more than shared custody? Should she believe he meant to stay? Maybe it wasn't only Leland who'd changed. But sometimes changes weren't permanent. Much as she'd love for this change to last, Saxon was a star. She'd witnessed him with his fans. He'd been in his element.

Heavens, how she wished she could gather the Artsy Ladies to share the fantastic news about the refuge, but they all led busy lives. At this rate it'd be time for the bazaar before they could all meet. But this news was too good not to share.

She stopped at the lane to her client's ranch and gathered everyone on a conference call. Jewell heard each friend pop on. Lila, sounding the most out of breath, asked, "What's up? Don't tell me Leland's taken a turn for the worse."

"No. You'll never in a million years guess. He deeded

me the forest for our refuge. Saxon says he won't let us pay anything."

For a second no one spoke. Then several squeals of delight filled her cab. "I suggested we name it the Conrad Snowy Owl Refuge. Is that okay?"

"Works for me," Tawana said. "By the way, Hunter is doing woodworking along with leather crafts. Shall I have him make us a couple of really nice signs? Maybe we can meet at the forest to post them after the bazaar. Jewell, do we need anything from the Natural Resources Committee to make this official?"

"Maybe paperwork. I'll check with them."

Myra broke in. "We need commemorative photos."

"That's what cell phones are for," Lila reminded.

"What'll we do with the money we've saved?" Mindy asked.

Shelley, who'd been silent, broke in. "Give it to Jewell to buy GPS tracking systems for the birds. She's paid for banding out of her pocket. But this year what we make at the bazaar, let's each keep."

It was agreed, and they chatted a bit about what items they had ready for the bazaar.

"Before we sign off," Lila called, "let's earmark some of what we earn to throw a bang-up baby shower for Myra. How about December 1?"

Her suggestion was met with enthusiasm.

"Don't you mean a shower for me and Jewell?" Myra asked. "We could wait until January even though I'm due around December 10."

"Don't wait," Jewell objected. "There'll be plenty of

time to hold a baby shower for me. I only had my first ultrasound."

"Okay," Tawana said. "But don't think we'll forget to celebrate your baby. I know you, Jewell—you like doing for others but don't like anyone doing for you. Get over it."

The friends all signed off and Jewell drove on through softly falling flakes, wondering if that was an accurate assessment of her. Was she too independent? Was that why she had distanced herself from Saxon, who said he wanted to coparent? She wanted to believe he would stay in town. Her heart beat faster brooding about it.

Too late to call Saxon as he'd requested when she got home, she headed to bed, where she poured her heart out to Shadow. "Saxon said everything he wants is here. Do you think he means me and our baby?"

The dog merely woofed.

THE NEXT MORNING Jewell hopped out of bed feeling some of her old verve. The light dusting of snow was melting in the crystal sunlight. Humming, she fed Shadow and flew around making breakfast burritos—enough to deliver some to Leland and Saxon. She was ready to open her heart and let him in—this time for good.

Half an hour later, arriving at Leland's ranch, she didn't see Saxon's SUV. Early as it was, she hoped that didn't mean Leland had had a relapse or anything.

Leland himself answered her knock. "Jewell, what

a nice surprise. Come in. Come in. What is it you have that smells so great?"

"Burritos. I hope egg and cheese is on your diet. Saxon said Doreen's been coaching him on cooking heart-healthy meals." She stepped inside and he closed the door. Warmth from his crackling fireplace enveloped her.

"Boring food, but I don't want more heart surgery. Doc Hamlin says I've got another fifty thousand miles on this repaired ticker. Let me get plates. Will you sit a spell and join me for breakfast? Coffee's fresh."

"Sure. I came to thank you for your generosity in giving us the land for the owls. Did Saxon tell you we'd like to name the refuge after you?"

"He did. That's nice but not necessary. I should've done it before." Leland set out two plates and got down another mug. "I must have been too sick to think straight."

She set the hot tray of burritos on the table and found a jar of salsa in his fridge. "Where is Saxon?" she asked, registering the table was set for two.

Leland pulled out a chair and sat. "He didn't call you this morning? Last night we were watching *The Late Show.* That agent fella called Saxon. It's something exciting but all hush-hush. Saxon couldn't say what, so he'll have to tell you."

"So, where is he?" she asked again, anxiety beginning to restrict her breathing.

"I 'spect he's in New York City by now. Somebody named Donovan arranged a red-eye out of Billings."

Leland picked up his fork and started to eat the steaming burritos.

Jewell felt as if the bottom had dropped out of her world. “He’s gone there to perform?” she asked woodenly.

“Yep, that’s part of it. I gathered it’s a big frickin’ deal.”

“Yesterday he swore he wouldn’t leave again. I took him at his word.”

Leland poured his coffee. “I can tell you it wasn’t an easy decision for him. In the end he said he owes the guy who gave him his first break in the music business.”

Jewell cut into her burrito. “I knew he’d never stay. He doesn’t fit in here.”

“Not so. He filled my woodshed and swabbed out this house from top to bottom. Yesterday afternoon he helped Eddie cover hay bales. I’ve gotta say I had my reservations, seeing how he opted out of ranch work as a kid. Truthfully, he’s been a godsend.”

“You raised him well.” Jewell picked up her burrito and polished it off.

“I can’t claim responsibility, since I was a grouch all the time he lived here. He’s a good man, Jewell. That’s all I’m gonna say. Well, I did consider using the forest to get you two together. Saxon made me see it was wrong. Maybe I’ll say one more thing. Yesterday he came in showing off that fuzzy picture of your little peanut. Proud, he is.” Leland paused to shovel in another bite.

“Peanut?” Jewell reached for a napkin.

“Well, he claimed it’s the baby. Looks like a peanut with skinny appendages.”

"That's my future child you're disparaging."

"My nephew's, too. Makes me related. Are you gonna give Saxon a chance?" He said it innocently enough, not looking up from cutting his next bite.

"Sorry, I have to go." Jewell stood up. "I'll be late checking Mark Watson's pregnant mare. The way he frets, you'd think his horse is the only one that's ever been artificially inseminated. Are you okay staying here alone?" she asked, rinsing off her plate and putting it in the dishwasher.

"Yep. Doreen's checking up on me until Saxon gets back."

"Whenever that is. If he returns, Sarah Jane wants him to sing at the Cattlemen's Association Christmas banquet. If he hasn't talked to her, would you remind him?" Bending, she gave the old man a quick hug and headed out.

"I appreciate breakfast," he called. "Tell Saxon yourself when he phones you."

"It's better he doesn't," she said, hardening her heart. "I suppose sometime we'll need to set rules for after I have the baby. But that's all, Leland."

"Aw, don't be like me. I wasted years being a lonely, grumpy old fool. Your brass ring is within reach. Grab it, girl."

Jewell didn't mean to let the front door slam. It did and she felt bad. Leland had mellowed since his surgery. He probably meant well. If anyone understood what it was like living with a broken heart, it'd be him. But her heart couldn't take any more of these roller-coaster ups and downs with Saxon.

Shivering, she climbed in her pickup. In a tiny corner of her mind she wondered if she was making a mistake writing him off. *No.* Losing Saxon the first time, the pain had been unbearable far too long. It was bound to be worse this time. This had to be the last time. A heart could break only so many times until it was unrepairable.

TWO HOURS LATER she was leaving the Watsons' barn when her cell rang. Pulling to the side of the road, she checked the readout and set it down as she saw it was Saxon. Then, cursing under her breath, she pulled herself together and answered.

"Jewell? I was about to hang up. Uncle Leland said you'd come by the ranch. He said you're mad at me. I meant to call when I landed at JFK, but Donovan was in a rush to drive me to Rockefeller Center, where I'm giving two shows tonight."

"That's nice. Sorry, I'm stopped at the side of the highway. I need to go."

"I can tell you're peeved. I swear this trip was totally unplanned. But I promise it's important to more people than me."

"I'm sure it is. I don't care, Saxon. I knew you wouldn't or couldn't give up performing. I'm going to ask Leland's lawyer to draw up some kind of custody agreement. You can tell him where he should send it later for your approval."

"Jewell. What the hell? I swear I'm coming back when this is over."

"Don't on my account. It's better if we keep our connection about the baby legal but long-distance. Visitations can be arranged through a third party."

"Dammit!" There was no mistaking Saxon's frustration. "Donovan's hollering. The band just arrived and I need to bring them up to speed on a couple of new songs. I have a week of shows, all ahead of… Well, I can't say. Just do me a favor. Next Saturday night, find the country music event on TV. It'll be on a major channel."

"I've seen you perform. I hope you've canceled with the kids expecting you to appear at their high school Christmas concert. Oh, and the Cattlemen's banquet if you arranged that with Sarah Jane Watson."

"You are so pigheaded. At the risk of sounding like the Terminator, I'll be back. Go and watch the country show with Leland."

Jewell heard his phone disconnect. She tossed hers in the passenger seat and drove off to her next appointment, her head aching.

Late that night it began to snow in earnest. Ranchers scrambled to cover cut hay and move cattle. Jewell kept super busy, too.

Saturday morning Doreen called her. "Are you coming to Leland's tonight to watch Saxon sing at that CMA award show? It's on at eight. I'm serving veggies and artichoke dip."

"Don't count on me. I'm worn out, Doreen."

"But you'll watch the show, right? Leland asked me to make sure."

"Maybe, unless I fall asleep first."

Jewell arrived home from her last job at seven. She

fed Shadow and heated soup for herself. Taking it into the living room, she lost the battle to ignore the show and turned on the TV. She scrolled through channels until she found the CMA Awards. She supposed in Saxon's world it was a big thing to appear at Madison Square Garden. And the announcer listed some huge stars. The first she realized just how big it was for Saxon was when his last single had a chorus played and a presenter indicated he was one of four performers up for Entertainer of the Year.

Glued to the TV, Jewell let her soup get cold. Near the end of the show, when the host shouted that Saxon had been voted by his fans to receive the prestigious Entertainer of the Year award, Jewell hugged Shadow and cried. And she cried. And cried harder when again Doreen phoned, bouncing-off-the-walls excited. "Honey, don't cry your eyes out. Saxon will be home Monday."

Pleased as Jewell was for him, she was more relieved her schedule was fully booked, because she knew after that win she'd lost him for good. His career had hit a new peak.

EVERYWHERE SHE WENT the whole week, all people wanted to talk about was Saxon winning the award. She operated by rote and avoided his calls.

For two full weeks she didn't answer him. When home, she made sure no lights were on in her house lest he get it in his head to stop by.

October ended in flooding rains. Jewell slopped through mud on a daily basis.

November dawned with spotty but cold sunshine.

Late that week Jewell ran into Tawana at the Tractor Supply Store. "Hey, did you hear Zeke and Myra lost a steer to a brown bear yesterday? Shelley's husband saw tracks in his area of the national park. He contacted Eddie, Aaron and Saxon. The guys all met Zeke and Seth to track the bear. As a ranger, Shelley's husband will tranquilize the animal, but he needed extra muscle to load him in a cage so they can haul him higher up into the mountains. Hunter wanted to go in the worst way but couldn't, because it's rough terrain and he does have the prosthetic."

"Saxon went?" Jewell set her feed sack on the counter. "I can't picture him out in the wilds."

Tawana delivered her an odd look. "Doreen said you're avoiding Saxon."

Jewell shrugged, and they parted without saying more.

Her days continued to be filled with work. Frankly, although it'd been her aim, she was hurt when Saxon stopped phoning her. She heard via the grapevine that the men had caught and relocated the bear. She'd also heard Saxon had agreed to sing at the Cattlemen's banquet. That meant he'd be around to the end of the year.

Downtime she spent fiendishly knitting hats, gloves and scarves for the bazaar. If they really kept the money from this year's sale, she'd invest hers in nursery furniture.

Days and nights passed, and her stomach began to pooch.

Not long before Thanksgiving, Lila phoned. "Hey, the Grange Hall is set up for the bazaar. I'm checking to see if all the Artsy Ladies want to take our projects there tomorrow around two-ish. I'll take coffee, tea and muffins. Once we're set up, we can discuss Myra's shower. Zeke offered to host it at their place. That way Myra won't have to load up gifts and drive home at night. Have you seen her? I swear she looks uncomfortable to even walk."

"That's what carrying twins will do. I'm finally seeing my baby bump. Nothing like Myra at this same stage in her pregnancy."

"With Rory I looked like I'd swallowed a basketball. You're so willowy maybe you won't gain much."

"I have another ultrasound tomorrow. Dr. Archer said it probably won't be until the one after this when I find out the baby's sex."

"Is Saxon getting anxious?"

"I've no idea."

"So...I promised myself I wouldn't bug you, but you know we'd all love to plan another wedding. Hint. Hint. We are approaching the season of miracles."

"If that miracle ever comes to pass, you'll be the first friend I call. But don't hold your breath."

"Sorry. But I must say, according to my husband, for a superstar, Saxon fits well with the men's group. They were happy campers tracking that bear. Oh, did Saxon tell you they all stopped to see the snowy owls and discussed where to fence and place the refuge signs Hunter's carving?"

"Lila...Saxon and I haven't spoken in weeks."

"That's a shame. I thought he wanted to be involved. Oops, I hear our new guests arriving. See you tomorrow afternoon at the Grange."

Jewell finished knitting a last scarf, then packed all her wares in a box. Outside, it was crisp and cold, but with no sign of snow like they'd dealt with last year.

Feeling restless, she called Shadow and took him for a walk around the property. Part of her restlessness came because she'd finally called to inform her folks that she was pregnant. At first her mom had freaked. Later she calmed down and sounded happy at the prospect of being a grandmother. So typical of her dad, he'd advised her to contact a lawyer and get every detail spelled out regarding custody and child support. When she'd insisted she didn't want or need any money from Saxon, her father casually pointed out how every year costs rose for clothing, athletics or things like dance and music lessons. Or proms and college tuition.

Her baby wouldn't even arrive until March. It seemed preposterous to talk about things like prom or college.

JEWELL WAS SHOCKED the next morning when she ran smack-dab into Saxon at the clinic. All the same, her heart puddled of its own accord. Right then she knew she'd been living a lie. She didn't want Saxon to leave. But from his stony expression, she wasn't sure how to begin to convince him to stay.

Eyeing her coolly, he said, "Leland's recheck with Dr. Hamlin fell at the same time Doreen said you're seeing Dr. Archer. We were across the hall."

One other patient sat in the waiting room reading on an electronic device. The nurse called her.

"Since you're here, it's okay if you want to go in for the ultrasound," Jewell said. "That is, if you'd like to."

"I would." He dropped into a chair as the nurse came for her.

"It's the same routine," she explained. "Once you're gowned and ready, Mr. Conrad can go back. By the way, congratulations on the CMA award." The nurse smiled at him.

He nodded.

"Yes, congratulations," Jewell murmured before rising to follow the nurse.

Leland walked in before anyone summoned Saxon. "Jewell didn't expect me, but she's letting me go in for the ultrasound. I'm not sure how long I'll be. By the way, what did Hamlin say?"

"He said I'm good to go about my normal business."

"So the pig valve you didn't want did the trick?"

Leland grimaced. "Must you remind me? I tell Doreen every time I catch myself snorting at the start of a laugh—check to see my nose hasn't turned into a snout."

Saxon laughed but glanced up as the nurse beckoned him. "Be right back," he told his uncle.

The picture had already come up on the screen. "How's everything?" he asked, moving to stand next to Jewell.

She sought his eyes. "Dr. Archer said I'm in tip-top shape. Can you see any specifics on the screen?" she queried, again studying the wavy lines.

"I know you two are anxious to learn the baby's gender. But the fetus is still curled a little tight. Normally we get a good, clear view at six months. I'm afraid you'll have to wait for your December visit."

Jewell sighed. "I'm disappointed. I'm meeting my women's group later to set up for the bazaar. I'd hoped to share if I'm having a boy or a girl." She brought up Myra's shower on December 1. "Is that too soon for me to come in again?"

"Yes. Sorry. Book closer to Myra's due date around the tenth, or we could even wait until after New Year's."

Jewell groaned and sat up. "My parents may come for Christmas. I'd like to tell them what I'm having. I know Mom will want to start buying everything in pink or blue."

Saxon touched her arm. "I didn't know your folks were coming. It'd be nice to see them. Leland and Doreen said to invite you to have Christmas dinner with us. Maybe we can all get together. Uh, think about it, okay? Uncle Leland's waiting in the outer room. Decide and let me know at the bazaar."

"How is Leland?" Jewell asked, holding her gown together in the back.

"Good. He said Dr. Hamlin gave him a green light to get on with his life. He's debating going to the bazaar. He said it's a big thing."

"It is. We started having the sale after you'd moved away. Parking is at a premium, Saxon. If you bring Leland, get there early so he doesn't have to walk so far."

"Since he's cleared by the doc to get on with his life, I assume he can walk as far as he likes."

Jewell frowned and pinched her lower lip. Did Leland's clean bill of health mean Saxon's time at the ranch was finally, truly nearing its end? She didn't know why that depressed her, since she'd been expecting it.

Chapter Twelve

Five minutes to two Jewell drove into the Grange parking lot and saw Hunter and Tawana unloading her car.

"Hi," she hailed them as she jumped out.

They waited for her to join them. "Here comes Lila," she said. "I wonder if Rory's class decorated the booths again this year."

"You'll be surprised and ecstatic when you see how everything is decorated this year," Tawana said.

"Oh?" Jewell jogged up the steps and pulled open the door. There were no turkeys and pumpkins as usual, but snowy owl cutouts everywhere. And lighted trees. "It's gorgeous. Who thought of this?"

Lila peered over her shoulder. "The middle school art teacher. The kids worked from your photos of our snowy owls."

Juggling her big box of knitted wear, Jewell spotted Hunter's booth. "Oh, I love that! Put a sold sticker on that rearing white stallion. He looks as if he'll explode right off the leather."

"Jewell, you should spend your money on the cute

baby sleep sacks I'm selling," Lila called from her booth.

"I'll buy from you, too—never fear."

The outer door squeaked open and they all turned to see who was coming in. Myra staggered in carrying one of her two-story dollhouses. Jewell and Lila ran to assist her.

"Myra, you shouldn't be lifting these," Lila scolded.

"Where's Zeke?" Hunter asked. He helped Jewell take the unwieldy house, but he wasn't yet fully steady on his prosthetic leg, so she bore the brunt of the weight.

Myra hunched over, hauling in deep breaths. "Zeke's mending a fence. We had a section down. Last night we heard wolves, so he had to repair it today. He told me not to bring the houses until he got home, but I wanted to be here with everyone. Oh. Oh!" Her face contorted and she grabbed her belly. "You guys, my water just broke. Lordy, I should've waited for Zeke. If the babies are coming, they're too early."

Jewell plunked down her end of the dollhouse and had her phone out calling the EMTs. "Dan and Ralph will be right here with an aid car to take you to the hospital."

"I'll have Zeke meet you there," Hunter said, taking out his phone.

"Breathe in and out slowly," Lila advised. "Are you in pain?"

"Some. I've had Braxton-Hicks contractions for two weeks. Who knew it'd be different today?"

They heard the siren and soon the firemen came in with a portable gurney.

Shelley and Mindy showed up with their wares, looking worried and confused when they had to jump aside to let the firemen pass.

"Did Myra fall? Is she okay?" Mindy asked.

Jewell explained that she was probably about to deliver her twins.

"The back of her pickup is full of dollhouses," Shelley pointed out. "Let's unload them and the rest of my ceramics. Myra's booth is between Mindy's and mine. We can handle her sales, too."

All agreed it would be a nice thing to do. But worry over Myra put a damper on their gathering. They drank the coffee Lila brought, but no one felt like eating muffins. Not until after Zeke phoned his twin, who put him on speakerphone, to say, "Hey, Seth, Myra and I are the proud parents of Emily and Jacob Maxwell. Tell everyone Mom and babies are doing great. The twins are almost five pounds each. Dr. Archer says that's exceptional. And they're beautiful. We can't wait to show them off."

"When can we visit?" the women chorused, nearly smothering Seth.

"This evening. Myra's worried about her dollhouses, though."

"Tell her the Artsy Ladies have her back there, so stop worrying," Seth assured his brother. Everyone's mood improved after he said goodbye. The rest of setup went smoothly, and the muffins got eaten.

THE FOLLOWING DAY the sale room buzzed with news of Myra and Zeke's bundles of joy. By then the friends had all seen the twins and pronounced them gorgeous.

What viewing the twins did for Jewell was make her long to hold her own baby. Watching how puffed up Zeke was as he moved through booths at the bazaar handing out pink and blue bubble gum totally demolished the barriers she'd erected around her heart about Saxon. She pictured him as a proud dad.

Off and on, Jewell glimpsed him talking to people and buying gifts. She was busy with a customer when he stopped by her booth to buy a knit hat and comment on the new arrivals. "Now I'm really anxious to know what we're having," she said.

He smiled. "That's the first time you've said *we*."

Her hand automatically flew to her belly. "Maybe because it's true. Saxon, I hate to ask a favor, but could you take that horse painting on leather out to my pickup? Hunter marked it sold, but a lot of ranchers are eyeing it. I don't want someone stealing it away." She started to get her pickup keys, but Saxon held up a hand.

"I'll put it in my SUV and bring it by tonight and help you hang it. That frame looks heavy."

"Thanks." She thought he was being extra nice, given how she'd been treating him. Guilt dogged her the rest of the day.

All the Artsy Ladies had sold out. At the end of the day as they cleaned up, they set a date to post Hunter's signs at the refuge. "I contacted the Natural Resources Committee chairwoman," Jewell said. "She's delighted we have land and will start the ball rolling to get our refuge federally approved."

On that note, the friends parted. Tired but happy, Jewell drove home. Almost at her house she noticed a set of headlights bouncing off her side-view mirror.

Stopping in front of the house, she climbed out and saw it was Saxon driving in. Waiting, she watched him retrieve her horse painting.

Inside, Shadow set up a ruckus.

"I'm beat," Jewell said, and dangled her house key. "Set the painting inside. We can hang it another day."

He didn't take the key. "I need a minute. I have news."

"Good or bad?" Jewell rubbed her lower back but quirked a brow.

"For you to decide."

Fear lanced through her when she saw his closed expression. Although she'd been preparing for him to announce his leave-taking, it hit like a gut punch to discover how badly she wanted him to stay. "I'll make coffee," she mumbled.

Her hand shook, but she managed to unlock the door and sidestep the leaping dog.

Saxon set the painting on the counter, then knelt to pet Shadow. "I'll feed him while you get coffee going."

"Don't drag it out, Saxon. Give me the news."

He glanced up from pouring kibble. "Today Leland asked Doreen Mercer to marry him."

Jewell gasped.

"She said yes."

His news was so far removed from what Jewell expected she dropped a full scoop of coffee grounds and had to clean up the mess. "I'm shocked. But why might I consider that news bad?"

"Maybe not for you. Bad for me. I'll have to buy a house or rent somewhere."

Her nerves, which had gone numb, tingled to life. "I know you're singing at a couple of Christmas events. Surely they won't get married until after New Year's."

Saxon screwed his lips to one side. "They want a Christmas Eve wedding. A small one. Doreen plans to ask your group to pull something together. Here's the bad part for you. They're pressuring for us to make it a double wedding."

This time Jewell counted too many scoops of grounds in the basket but drew the water and turned the maker on anyway.

"Yes," she said firmly, gripping the edge of the counter as she faced him.

He stopped rolling the top down on the kibble bag. "Yes, what?"

"If you're asking…will I go along with a double wedding, my answer is yes. Unless you object." She gazed at him from hopeful, watery eyes.

Saxon tossed the kibble bag into the pantry and yanked her into his arms. "Yes, yes, yes, I'm asking… begging," he said, covering her upturned face with kisses. "I thought you were mad at me. I thought you wanted me to leave. But…Jewell, I told Uncle Leland they're meddling busybodies. We can do something on our own later if your dream wedding is for something bigger."

"Sooner is better. I thought I was going to have to find a way to propose to you," she finally got out breathlessly. "I just…want us to be together and make a family when our baby comes. Honestly, I've been all over the map, wanting you to leave and scared to death you would. While you were in New York, Leland said I should grab the brass ring and not end up an old grump like he was for so long. I was afraid. I've sent you away twice. It'd serve me right if you went and told me to go jump in the lake."

"I love you, Jewell. I always have."

She touched his face. "I've been a fool not to see that as much as I love this town and people, I love you more. When you tour again, after our baby is born, we'll go with you," she promised in a rush. "I'll have someone cover my practice. We'll make it work."

"I'm done touring, babe."

"But…you just got that big award."

"No better time to go out than when you're on top. Prepare to get sick of seeing me hanging around plunking on my guitar while I write songs. I'm ready to be a househusband and full-time babysitter, sweetheart."

"Really?" She slipped her arms around his neck. Pure joy filled her as they made plans while the coffee perked.

BY THE NEXT day word of both weddings sped like wildfire through the grapevine. Jewell's friends were over the moon, as were Doreen's.

"Myra's mom is coming to see the babies. She'll sew your dress, as well as Mom's," Lila informed Jewell. “If you imagined wearing blue jeans, no way. We chose green velvet for you and red for my mom. A festive Christmas Eve wedding.”

“Great, we’ll look like Santa’s elves.”

“Quit grumbling. It’s out of your hands. Mindy found the rest of us simple winter-white knit dresses with long sleeves at an online outlet. They’re ordered and should arrive by the tenth, the day Myra was supposed to have her twins.”

“That’s the day we’re dedicating the refuge,” Jewell said. “And the day Saxon and I hope to learn if we’re having a boy or a girl.”

“No better way to close out a super year.”

“On that score, I agree,” Jewell said, content at last.

THE DAYS AFTER she and Lila spoke passed swiftly. Doreen wanted to bake their wedding cake—double hearts. But her new employee at the café wrested the chore out of her hands.

Saxon and his uncle did their best to stay out of everyone’s way. Then on December 10 he and Jewell went to see Dr. Archer.

The doctor and her nurse congratulated the pair on their upcoming nuptials, which earned them invitations to the Christmas Eve double ceremony at the Owl’s Nest.

“I’ll be out of town,” Dr. Archer said. “But first let’s see what shows on this ultrasound.” She ran the wand over Jewell’s rounded belly and the infant appeared onscreen seeming to wave a hand.

Jewell and Saxon were so transfixed they almost missed a view showing they were going to have a daughter. When Dr. Archer pointed it out, Saxon clasped his soon-to-be wife's left hand—on which he'd placed a beautiful emerald engagement ring, one Seth Maxwell, the former gem hunter, had rounded up. Kissing Jewell's palm, Saxon said with feeling, "I hope she has your red hair."

"I hope she has your talent," Jewell responded as the doctor printed copies of the picture of their baby.

Dr. Archer smiled. "She'll be perfect. Go book an appointment for in the New Year."

They went to do that hand in hand.

THAT AFTERNOON THE friends met at the forest. The men strung a mesh fence, then set Hunter's signs. The women oohed over them, and over Jewell's ultrasound photo. All at once fat snowflakes began to drift from clouds occluding the mountains. Three snowy owls flew down to silently circle the group as if giving their blessing. Linking arms, they all happily watched the gorgeous birds.

SCANT WEEKS LATER the Christmas Eve weddings went off without a hitch even on a snowy day. Before the ceremony, the minister christened Zeke and Myra's twins.

After the couples' vows, Leland hugged Doreen and prepared to give a champagne toast, except with apple juice for Jewell.

"To my lovely bride and to my nephew and his. I will always consider this day icing on a long-awaited cake."

"I consider it a true season of miracles," Jewell said, nudging Lila, who'd once mentioned that very thing.

Saxon raised his glass, then hugged Jewell and added his pledge. "Sweetheart, for the rest of our lives I'm going to write and sing you all the love songs you inspire."

There was no mistaking a collective sigh shared by beaming guests.

* * * * *

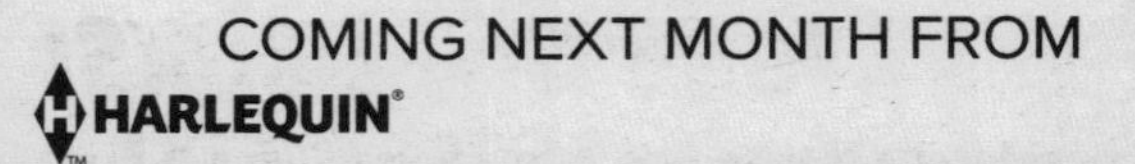

Western Romance

Available January 3, 2017

#1625 HER COLORADO SHERIFF

Rocky Mountain Twins • by Patricia Thayer

Newly hired as interim sheriff of Hidden Springs, Colorado, Cullen Brannigan plans to move into a house on the family ranch...except he finds it's already occupied by Shelby Townsend and her five-year-old nephew!

#1626 A VALENTINE FOR THE COWBOY

Sapphire Mountain Cowboys
by Rebecca Winters

Rancher Eli Clayton is raising his little fourteen-month-old daughter, Libby. When he sees her happily ensconced in the arms of a beautiful stranger, he begins to wonder if his daughter needs a mommy...and if he needs a wife!

#1627 THE BULL RIDER'S COWGIRL

Men of Raintree Ranch • by April Arrington

When easy-living bull rider Colt Mead becomes his young sister's guardian, he needs Jen Taylor's help. But it will take more than friendship to convince the determined barrel racer to give up her race for glory.

#1628 RODEO FATHER

by Mary Sullivan

Cowboy Travis Read has always been a loner. But when he meets Rachel McGuire, the pregnant widow and her daughter make him believe being part of a family might be possible after all!

YOU CAN FIND MORE INFORMATION ON UPCOMING HARLEQUIN® TITLES, FREE EXCERPTS AND MORE AT WWW.HARLEQUIN.COM.

HWESTCNM1216

Could a second chance at happiness be around the corner for Shelby Townsend when brooding Sheriff Cullen walks into her life?

Read on for a sneak preview of HER COLORADO SHERIFF, the third book in Patricia Thayer's stunning quartet ***ROCKY MOUNTAIN TWINS.***

Hearing the feminine voice, Cullen swung around to find Shelby standing in the doorway. She looked fresh and pretty dressed in her jeans and blouse. Her rich brown hair was pulled back into a ponytail. She was ready for work at the café.

"Sorry, I knocked, and I heard you…" She paused. "I just wanted to tell you that… Never mind." She frowned. "I can see that this isn't a good time. I'll come back later."

When she started to leave, he hurried after her. "Wait." He caught her hand. "Don't go, Shelby. It's not you. In fact, you're just what I need right now." When he tugged on her hand it caused her to stumble right into his arms. He saw her surprise, her rapid breathing, but more than that, those eyes, blue depths, held passion. And he wanted her.

"Cullen?"

Her saying his name broke the last of his resistance. He lowered his head and brushed his lips across hers. He was quickly becoming lost. His mouth moved over hers gently, and when she didn't resist, he wrapped his arms around her and held her close.

Oh, God. She felt wonderful. Her taste, her softness and that sexy body… He tilted her head, getting a better angle to deepen the kiss. She moaned and her hands moved to his chest, and he burned. He wanted more. He cupped her face and kissed her deeper. Then reluctantly, he ended the kiss and released her. He watched her blink those startling blue eyes, and he almost went back for more. Instead he slipped his hands into his pockets and said, "Wow! I didn't mean to do that… Did you want to ask me something?"

She opened her mouth and paused as if to clear her head. "Huh, I just was going to offer to help you with the horses." She couldn't look him in the eyes. "Look, I should go. Ryan's in the car."

He started to argue, then stopped. "Okay."

She nodded. "I'll see you later." She turned and walked out the back door. He watched her until she got into her car and drove off.

"Well, that was just great, Brannigan. Talk about overstepping your boundaries."

How was he going to fix this?